HER LADY'S WHIMS AND FANCIES

Lords for the Sisters of Sussex

JEN GEIGLE JOHNSON

Lords for the Sisters of Sussex Series

Follow Jen's Newsletter for a free book and to stay up to date on her releases. https://www.subscribepage.com/y8p6z9

Follow Jen

Jen's other published books

The Nobleman's Daughter
Two lovers in disguise

Scarlet
The Pimpernel retold

A Lady's Maid
Can she love again?

His Lady in Hiding
Hiding out at his maid.

Spun of Gold
Rumplestilskin Retold

Dating the Duke
Time Travel: Regency man in NYC

Charmed by His Lordship
The antics of a fake friendship

Tabitha's Folly
Four over protective Brothers

To read Damen's Secret
The Villain's Romance

Follow her Newsletter

Prologue in Which June Standish Receives her Wedding Gift.

Kate Standish, the second youngest of five Standish sisters, held a letter with shaking hands as the words blurred in front of her. She blinked furiously. Even happy tears caused red-rimmed eyes, and she could be nothing but perfectly beautiful on her sister's wedding day. They would have to cry all their happy tears together. She read through her letter again. And now to receive this news.

June was so deserving of every happiness. Kate's new and first brother by marriage would be Lord Morley. Could they be anymore blessed? Their broken-down old castle looked more beautiful every day. They had been enjoying full meals on the table and even a modiste for new gowns, two things that Kate wondered if they would ever have again. The reason for her work on *Her Lady's Whims and Fancies* fashion plates, and for this most recent letter. And now, to receive such news when the direst need had truly passed—or had it? She would have to consider carefully. For Kate would never, ever go hungry again, not she or any she loved.

But today was a day for celebrations. She grinned. And

hoped. Though June had tried to keep the wedding small, Lady Morley—soon to be dowager—had been determined to throw the largest wedding Brighton had ever seen. Perhaps she was hoping to make amends for her abhorrent interference in June and Morley's courtship?

The castle was full to bursting.

Kate exited the family wing of their home. She was dressed and ready. Her hair done up in the very latest fashion. She'd drawn up a fashion plate of the style just yesterday and sent it off to the paper. One advantage to drawing the plates herself? She would be wearing the very style *The Morning Sun* touted as the latest fashion, before anyone else saw it. She smiled to herself.

One additional change Kate thought she'd never have again was the entrance of five lady's maids, one for each of the sisters. Kate's was a talented young woman named Hannah, who was studying all the magazines and papers she could find for ideas on what hairstyle they could create together.

A few doors down the hall, Amelia stepped out of her bedroom; the sounds of a baby laughing behind her in the room followed her out.

Kate's heart swelled. "Good morning to you, Your Grace." She curtseyed.

"Oh, Amelia, please. When we are here at home just us, please call me Amelia."

"I don't want to slip up and use your name when there are others around. Lucy might cut off my braid in my sleep."

"She would never do such a thing." Amelia laughed. "Though she might be tempted."

Kate's sister Lucy found every reason to be immersed in the world of the nobility. She studied them, knew all their forms of address, and corrected the others for any impropriety. If that sister didn't marry a rising duke, Kate would be shocked.

"How is sweet Peter this morning?"

Amelia's face softened even more, and she smiled. "Gerald and Richard are in there playing with him right now. I will admit, it is one of the sweetest scenes I have yet to see."

"I'm so happy for you." Kate stepped closer and embraced her friend. Amelia had come to their family with her new husband, The Duke of Granbury, right when they had needed him most desperately.

They moved down the stairs in search of breakfast together. Amelia wrapped her hands around Kate's arm. "You look beautiful. There will be talk of which of all the Standish sisters is the most beautiful. I'm certain no one will be able to decide."

"June, certainly, as she is the bride. I haven't seen her yet this morning."

"I think Morley left rather late last night."

Kate smiled. "He is better than I would have imagined for our dear June."

"Yes, Morley is the second best man that I know."

Kate smiled. "Soon, he might be relegated to fourth."

"To fourth, you say?" Morley had just stepped in the front door.

"What are you doing here? It's not right to see the bride before the wedding." Kate stepped forward and embraced her almost brother-in-law.

"I won't even look at her. But I couldn't stay in that inn one moment longer knowing that everyone I hold dear in the world would be here at the castle." He leaned forward and kissed Amelia's cheek. "And how are my two godsons?"

"Up creating havoc on the bed with their father."

"And all in the world is right where it should be." He cleared his throat and eyed the staircase enough that Kate laughed. "Would you like me to fetch June for a moment?"

"If you could. I have a wedding present." His eyes shone with so much hope and love, Kate couldn't refuse him.

"Oh, very well. I shall see if she is available." She laughed to herself as she ran back up the stairs.

She entered the corridor where all of their bedrooms lined the hallway. Her sisters' friendly chatter coming from the room at the end of the hall made her smile. Were they all together in June's room?

As she entered, Kate's eyes welled again, and this time, she did nothing to stop the tears. June stood in front of her mirror, a white gown shimmering and billowing all around her in lovely folds that fell to the floor. June had let her design the dress, and Kate had given the modiste very specific instructions and drawings. Between the two of them, the dress had turned out perfectly.

Her other sisters—Charity, Lucy, and Grace—came and stood at Kate's side. Charity handed Kate a handkerchief. "Doesn't she look beautiful?"

Kate nodded and dabbed her eyes. "June." She ran to her sister and squeezed her tight. "You are just exquisite."

The other sisters gathered round, and soon, they were in one hug, all together, laughing and wiping their eyes.

"Mother would have loved this day." June dabbed at her own eyes and then smiled at them all. "Could we be so blessed?"

Each sister shook their heads. And Kate remembered her purpose. "Morley is downstairs."

June's face lit to a happiness Kate could not even imagine for a person.

"He says he has a wedding gift."

"Should we invite him up?" June's eyes danced with mischievous merriment.

"It will soon be his set of rooms as well as yours." Grace shrugged.

"Technically, they already are his set of rooms." Charity huffed just a touch and then laughed. "Oh, let him up."

"I will tell him!" Grace ran from the room, and though she was already fourteen, Kate loved the easy, innocent manners of the youngest of her sisters.

"Does anyone else but me remember that it is bad luck for the groom to see the bride? Or that this is her bedchamber? Or . . ."

"No, Lucy, none of us remember." Charity put her arm across Lucy's shoulders. "It's Morley. Our brother needs us to celebrate with him as well as June."

"He did say he was lonely at the inn when all he loved were here at the castle," Kate said.

"Truer words never spoken." Morley stood in the doorway, and Kate admitted just a little swoon on behalf of her sister, who looked like she was swooning enough for all of them. He stood tall, in a dark coat, his cravat crisp and white and perfectly knotted. His jawline sharp. His hessians were the newest style and shined so much that she wanted to peer over and see if her reflection was visible. He was also using an interesting type of button. It reflected some of the sunlight in the room in a dark, shiny manner, and she found herself wanting to touch one of them. A lovely gold chain hung from one pocket to presumably a tucked-in pocket watch. His rings—just two, a signet and another gold band—fit his fingers just right. As Kate's gaze travelled over all his presentation, she decided yet again that Lord Morley was perfect for her sister June.

He entered, with eyes only for June. He carried a box in his hands, small, blue. "For you."

The sisters gathered closer.

"I think you will all appreciate this." Morley nodded at June. "Open it."

She lifted the cover and then sucked in a breath, tipping it so that everyone could see.

Kate's heart flipped over inside. "Are those the jewels from William the Conqueror?"

"The very ones. I've had them reset. And I think this sapphire is perfect for June's dinner this evening. Don't you?" he turned to ask Kate, and she stood taller. "Yes, they will be amazing with her dress."

"They are yours. I've had all the jewels either reset or strengthened in their original settings. It is only right that you sisters have them."

"Thank you, Nicholas." June stepped closer, and the sisters faded away.

Grace giggled into her hands. "Does it bother anyone else when she calls him Nicholas?"

"He's Morley to me." Kate shrugged.

"*Lord* Morley really." Lucy turned away as Morley kissed June.

Kate looked over her sisters. "Have you told your maids the instructions for your hair?"

"Yes." Lucy nodded. "We need to look like we fit in with . . . the nobility."

"I modified your instructions somewhat." Charity lifted her eyebrows as though she knew what Kate was about to say.

"Modified it to what?" Kate shook her head. "It wouldn't hurt you to be perfectly and completely in the mode for once— this day particularly, as all of the ton is likely to show up."

"Yes, thanks to Mother. It won't be too much of a hardship, I'm sure." Morley winked at them. "I have heard of a few perhaps notable attendees." He dipped his head at Lucy. "The almost Duke of Kently, Lord Tanner."

Lucy's eyes lit, and she tried to hide her reaction, but her face burned a bright pink.

"And . . ." He turned to Kate. "Lord Dennison."

Her throat caught. How could he know of her interest in Lord Dennison?"

"Um . . . who?" She tried to appear uncaring.

"As if you don't know of the most fashion-conscious lord in all of England. Well, perhaps besides Beau Brummel and his set, but Lord Dennison, it is said, is somewhat of a protégé of Brummel himself."

"Oh, yes." Kate nodded. Of course, everyone had heard of him.

Morley studied her for a moment. "You are excited to see him, I presume, if anything, just to take note of how he dresses?"

Kate forced a laugh. "Of course."

"And now, I must check in on Gerald and his lads." He bowed to them all. With one last look at June, he was out the door.

Charity turned back to her sisters. "I have no desire to be completely in the mode, as you call it. I don't mind adding a touch of myself, if you know what I mean."

Kate opened her mouth to tell her that she must not do such a thing, but June clapped her hands. And her huge smile stopped all other conversation. "This is really happening, my sisters."

They gushed and loved each other, and Kate noted how each of their gowns was exquisite, down to the smallest detail. June had asked her to oversee such things.

Once the sisters were finished with their hair, Charity even succumbing to the maid and Kate's attempts to fashion her hair in a large, cascading mound of curls on the top of her head, Kate took a moment in her room.

She reread the letter.

We are pleased to inform you that all of your next drawings have been accepted for this month's Whims and Fancies. We look forward to what you might send for next month. As discussed, we would also like to offer you a space for your thoughts on the fashion of the day, who was seen wearing what, and what you predict will become on mode shortly. This would be a columnist position, and we would expect a weekly on-dit from you.

Tonight would not be all about June, no. For Kate, tonight was also about research.

And, as Morley had informed her, Lord Dennison would be there. She'd watched Lord Dennison from afar, for a long time. There was something about the ton's fascination with his daring fashion choices, his visits to certain families over others, his appearances at balls. She watched for him in every bit of the weekly gossip columns, as if trying to make him out. In part because of one bit of gossip she read. The day Lord Dennison was the only man to dance with Wallflower Willow. Whoever that was. The paper had made note that he had asked her to dance, not once, but twice, and soon, her card had filled.

So now, Kate wanted to know what motivated such a man. She wanted to see what he wore and how he did his hair, of course. *Her Lady's Whims and Fancies* would eat up any information she had about Lord Dennison—unnamed, of course—but she could never claim her interest in him was solely to appease the gossips. Not when she'd ended many a day wondering what color were his eyes.

Chapter One

Lord Logan Dennison lifted his chin to allow for one more fold of fabric at his neckline. This new knot would be the rage of London in two weeks' time, when Logan would move on to another. Although, this might be his favorite knot so far. It just looked . . . regal.

But his valet had a devil of a time learning how to do the intricate folds and ties and keeping the various degrees of crispness to the material.

"Wiggins. You have outdone yourself."

"Thank you, my lord." His nimble fingers created the final touches, and at last, the two-hour ministrations were at an end.

Wiggins brushed down the jacket again, tugging at the lines and his sleeves, and then he stood back, eyeing his hessians. "They are shined to perfection."

Logan turned, appreciating the lines, the straight jacket, and most of all, his hair. "This style. Let us hope too many others do not copy it all at once. I'd like to linger here for a time."

"Yes, it suits you." Wiggins nodded. "You are ready, if I do say so."

"I shall return to prepare for the dinner hour and ball this evening. We are off to the church to see some poor chap tie his own knot, in an endless noose of matrimony."

"Very good, my lord."

Logan was to sit near the front. He and his sister and mother had been invited by Lady Morley. He joined them in the carriage. "Been waiting long?"

"No. We just sat in this moment." His twin sister, Julia, eyed his cravat. "Still wearing the Croatian?"

"Well, it is my own invention. I thought it fitting to wear it more than one time at least."

"How long do you think it will take before any of the others attempt it?"

He lifted his chin. "As if their valets could manage such a thing. It took Wiggins two hours to tie this masterpiece."

"It is quite the thing, really." She leaned closer. "Seems incredibly complicated. Not at all simple like the Mathematical, or the Oriental. Those seem so outdated now that you and your set walk around with these newer demonstrations." She unfolded a paper and began to read.

"What are you reading?"

Julia lifted up the paper to show him. "The latest copy of *Her Lady's Whims and Fancies.*"

"Oh?" Logan adjusted his sleeves. "And what does it instruct this week?"

"She offers drawings—four fashion plates." She lifted the paper to show him.

"Forward-thinking." He studied the dresses and then nodded, approvingly. "Just fashionable enough to reach the current trend, but daring enough to urge people forward."

She studied him. "Like your cravat."

"Precisely." He pointed a lazy finger at her paper. "Surely designed by a man."

"How can you say that? As if a man knows the finer intricacies of women's fashion?"

"And why shouldn't he? Do you not dress as you do to find yourself a man?"

She huffed, and he smiled. "You know I'm in jest. At least, somewhat."

"How can you pretend such a thing? I dress how I want to dress to please the ladies at Almacks." She laughed.

"For those old bats?"

His mother clucked. "Must you call them something so impolite?"

"Oh, too true, Mother. I don't wish to insult your friends."

Julia shuddered in mock horror. "They scare me. I live in fear they will reject my voucher."

"Well, no one will keep you from the church, you can count on that. And we are almost arriving." Their townhome off The Strand in Brighton was not far from the church.

"I'm so looking forward to this wedding. How romantic. Can we discuss how they met?" Julia said.

"Certainly. Quite absurd, in my mind. His Grace, the Duke of Granbury, lost a property in a card game, but he didn't tell his best friend about the lovely tenants to go along with it." Logan thought that devilishly hard of a friend to do to another.

"And then he fell in love with the eldest." Julia turned to their mother. "Is that not the most romantic story of our age?"

"Certainly, dear. Though I don't wish for you to be about getting your husband in that manner. It's not quite bad ton precisely. They are of the royal family, after all. Distantly." She sniffed. "However, it would not behoove us to follow such an example."

"Mother. We will never be in a situation where Logan is gambling away our home." Julia fanned her face. "Unseasonably warm."

They had entered a line of carriages and were moving slowly toward the church.

"This is the party of the year. Lady Morley made certain of it. You can thank me for our invitations." Logan's mother looked so pointedly at him, he had to exert real effort not to express his extreme dislike at having to attend at all.

"Perhaps the almost dowager hopes not to be sent to the northern estate after all." His sister snickered. "I've heard stories of the way she treated those sisters. When everyone else says they are perfectly lovely."

"How you know the things you do, I'll never guess," Logan said.

She held up her paper. "Right here. There's an on-dit where we read the latest gossip—no names, of course. And then the fashion plates. Heavens. I'd never know anything if I didn't read it."

"And I thought all the good news filled the betting books at Whites." He'd been victim to their merciless jabs once news of Olivia had reached the ton's ears.

"Heavens, no. That's just you men being silly. The real information is right here. You just have to read between the lines a bit sometimes to decipher who is who." Julia tapped her chin. "They mention you at least three times every week."

"Do they?" His interest was piqued. "Advertising my latest cut, no doubt?"

"Not at all. They are much more interested in the things you say. Or one time, there was a whole piece about why you did not ask Lady Alastair to dance."

"That's what they care to write about? Perhaps I was tired, perhaps she was retiring early—there are so many influences as to why a man might do things."

"But in this instance, she was standing nearby. You were

free, and so was she, but instead of dancing, you took yourself to get a lemonade." Julia dipped her chin. "And that is news."

He looked from Julia to his mother and back. "I hardly find that riveting."

"And yet?" She held up the paper. "Now the speculation is that you shall at last find your heart at the wedding party of Morley and Miss Standish."

"Not likely."

Of course, now his mother would pipe up. "Oh come, son. Don't you think it is high time you marry?"

"Marry? High time?" He braced himself for more comments like this one, and for others, their heartless speculation about how his broken heart might one day mend barely endurable on a good day.

They stopped at last in front of the church. Logan stepped out of the carriage, breathing the freedom of air in which no one was urging him to choose a wife, and then he turned to hand down his sister and mother.

They each took an arm, and the three made their way into the church. He braced himself. *She* would be here somewhere, in the very church where he'd proposed like a lovesick ninny, a weak-lipped idiot. His gaze flicked to the front, the sanctuary where the vicar stood. If he looked closer, Logan would see the scratch in the stone, scuff marks, and a discoloration right where his knees had rested, where he held out his hand with his mother's ring, and where Olivia had denied him.

He looked away. Why relive such a moment? But his eyes flitted immediately to the back of the head of the other member of the memory. He knew it was her—even with the mobcap of the married, even with another man's arm around her shoulders, he would know her anywhere.

Logan resisted straining against his cravat. That would only leave an unwelcome space between his neck and the material, causing the whole knot to sag.

With his sister and mother on each arm, he walked to the front of the church and sat in the third row, reserved for the Marquess of Dennison. He knew every eye was on him. He knew hers must be as well. And he knew he looked like the paragon he was. Lord Dennison, the Marquess of Dennison, Magistrate as well as Baron of Hampton, as well as an active member of the House of Lords, Whig leader, fashion paragon, and not to mention, overall charming person. He sat precisely, telling himself all the eyes on him was a good thing, and waited for the wedding to begin.

Julia scooted as close as she could. "There they are." In her lap, almost hidden by the folds of her skirts, her finger deftly pointed out a row of women to their front.

He hadn't yet looked at a single other person in the great cathedral. He meant to follow the direction of Julia's finger to appease her and then glance away, but his attention was caught by the woman directly to his front. Her hair was lovely, dark, shiny. Each of the women on their row had magnificent hair, honestly. Evidence that they were no longer destitute relatives to be passed from one family to another was in their whole presentation. Their dresses were new, their gloves crisp and white. All women's gloves were white, but they were only crisp for the first few months of wear.

His attention returned to the woman directly at his front. Her neck. Lovely soft skin. The curls adorning her creamy skin were perfectly formed and looked as though they would spring back at his touch. And the piece at the top. She gave almost the impression of wearing a crown. And he was quite enchanted by her whole appearance. The neckline was lined with jewels and lace, and the braided effect of ribbon handled so expertly that his eyes naturally traced it. *Well done*. She had created a master-piece. He must know her designer.

His attention was pulled away by the beginnings of the cere-mony. He braced himself for the hurt he knew would come.

As soon as Lord Morley had agreed to love the new Lady Morley and none else as long as he lived on the earth, the congregation stood as the new, overly happy couple hurried down the aisle together and out to a crowd of cheering people.

Logan murmured at the top of Julia's head, "His cravat could have been something more creative. But her dress. It was perfection. I hope you took note."

Julia nodded as though she only half-heard. She'd begun chat-tering away with their mother about every person in the room.

A set of eyes burned his side, and before he could stop himself, he turned, then cursed his distraction.

Olivia stared large and doe-like eyes right at him.

Her husband nodded his head, once.

But her expression was almost soulful, asking. What did she want from him? He almost snorted. Nothing he was willing to give. He schooled his featured and looked away without any reaction. He had no mind to give attention to married women who had rejected all he had to offer.

Two other women on the same row, with similar wistful expressions, eyed him. That was the trouble with weddings. It put every female mind in the mode of marrying. He'd best escape as soon as he dared.

Logan forced his eyes to the front. Every sister in the row to his front had handkerchiefs out, dabbing their eyes. Their row moved to exit together while he waited. His gaze flickered to the woman with the fascinating hair. Her eyes were squarely on him, and when she had his attention, she curtseyed, watching him, before she followed her sisters.

"She's so beautiful," Julia whispered at his side. "Which sister is that? She's absolutely stunning. And that hair. Did you see she is wearing the very style that the plates suggest is coming *next month*? And the turn of her nose."

Julia's voice continued in his ear, but it was lost as he had similar yet more elevated thoughts race around in his mind, disturbing his peace. Thoughts that were a risk to his happiness, thoughts that led men to do simplistic, half-crazed things like propose to women of her ilk. "Stop."

Julia paused mid-sentence. "Pardon me?"

"She's fine. She's pretty. She's just like every other woman here—cares nothing for anyone but herself, wrapped up in her own presentation, with probably naught but straw in her head."

Julia gasped, and then she turned to watch the sisters still moving their way out of the row.

The very sister in question had stiffened, and her face colored with a blotchy pink. As she lifted her chin in the picture of defiance, Logan suspected she had heard him.

"Oh no."

"Yes, she might have heard you, brother. Keep your bitter wool-gathering to yourself. Do you wish to hurt feelings?"

"No. I don't." His heart clenched before he, too, raised his chin. "But if she wouldn't pay such close attention where she is not acquainted, she wouldn't be hearing things not meant for her ears."

Julia just shook her head. "I don't know how you're going to mend that, but you best. On the day of her sister's wedding." Her eyes bore into his.

He knew she was correct. And he felt guilty, yes. But more than anything, he was annoyed at the inconvenience. He had been planning to spend his evening doing exactly as he pleased, parading his new jacket, embroidered for this very occasion.

Chasing after a woman to help mend feelings that might not need mending had not been a part of his plans.

"Let's get you home before you punch something," Julia said.

"As if I ever punch things."

"Perhaps you should. Jacksons might be just the thing."

"Well, remind me when we have returned to London. Until then, I best keep myself firmer in control."

Her soft sigh made him study her face. "What is this?" Logan asked.

"Or . . . Perhaps you need to let go . . . of things. I miss you —the real you."

He considered her words as they returned to their carriage. He supposed she was referring to Olivia. "Instead, I think I shall wear a new pair of slippers this evening." They were colorful and pointy, and every person in the room would be shocked by them. He smiled. "Yes. That will be just the thing."

"If you say so." She lifted her paper back up to her face. "At least it will give me something interesting to read about next week."

And something besides Olivia for him and all the others to talk about.

Chapter Two

Kate smiled and laughed with her sisters, trying desperately to not let the words of one man ruin what should be the happiest day of their lives so far. But ouch, his words stung. And echoed some of the reaction she received even from her sisters. No one considered her interest in fashion to be anything but frivolous. If she had spent the same amount of time gushing over needlepoint or painting, they would have cheered her talents, but fashion just felt inconsequential. To them.

Little did they know she had begun this path as a way to keep them all from starvation. Bitterness tinged the air as she threw flower petals high into the sky.

And of all people to make that comment. Lord Dennison? The fashion king of the ton? How dare he pass judgement. His cravat was nothing short of ridiculous. It was one thing to design a new knot that added to his appearance, and quite another to distract her eye from his appearance to focus solely on the space below his chin. If he were wise, he'd be drawing attention upward into his face. His jawline and on up to his strong nose and eyes . . .

Her traitorous stomach leapt. No matter how handsome, his words had given window to his heart, and she wanted none of that. Whether or not she could learn from such a man, from his own ridiculous focus on fashion, she would watch from afar and send her opinion to *Whims and Fancies* in the morning.

Her fingers itched to start drawing. Perhaps for the first time, she could do a satire. She laughed to herself as she imagined an overly large, towering mass of white bursting forth from below his chin. The next image of him, trying to see around the massive cravat in his face. Her laughter added to the joy around them, and Grace clung to her arm. "Isn't this wonderful?!"

"Yes. Oh, it really is."

June and Morley climbed into their carriage and waved. She blew kisses to the sisters. Kate wished to catch one and hold it close. "When do they return?" she asked.

"Not for a month." Grace's pout immediately brought Kate's arm across her shoulders.

"We shall try to endure it."

"And is His Grace staying with us?"

"I believe so. He and Amelia have said as much."

"Oh, I am pleased."

"And we have Charity."

They both turned to watch their sister. She was in high debate already about something with two men standing at her side.

"Oh, dear. Perhaps we should make our way home?" Grace's face pinched.

"Yes, I do believe we should." Kate laughed. "Nothing to worry about of course. This is our Charity."

A handsome man bowed over Lucy's hand.

"Who is that?" Grace was watching the same scene.

"Is that . . ." Kate squinted.

Charity joined them. "She's done it. She's finally met the almost Duke of Kently."

Kate studied him. "He's not as finely dressed as I would have imagined."

"Of course, you'd say that." Charity sniffed. "There are other things to care about than one's manner of dress."

"I know, Charity. It is merely an observation."

Her words stung. But Kate tried to remember her words said more about Charity than Kate. The woman tried as hard as she could to diminish the importance of her own appearance for reasons Kate could not understand. But Charity loved fiercely, and Kate would stand by her no matter what she wore. She smiled. "Sisters. It's just four now."

"Not forever. They'll be back." Grace frowned.

They climbed into their new carriage. "Right. We haven't lost a sister, just gained a brother."

Lucy joined them, breathless. "So they say. But surely, that's true for us. Morley is excellent."

They started to move. Charity crossed her arms. "Tell us. You've met the almost duke."

"His name is Lord Tanner."

"But all that matters about him so far is his title." Charity's eyebrows rose in challenge.

Lucy sighed. "I know." She looked out the window and said nothing more. "I admit, he was not everything I've hoped."

"But he might grow on you."

"Perhaps."

Kate felt her energy rise. A few hours more, and they could make their entrance to the ball. "Sisters . . . ball gowns. They are exquisite. I cannot wait for everyone to see us."

Lucy moved closer to her. Grace and Charity smiled.

Charity nodded. "I can't wait for the duchesses to see us."

"That's very vain-sounding for you, Charity." Kate laughed.

"You know how I feel about their nose-in-the-air condescension. I cannot abide one more meeting in our front room where we are counseled yet again on the blessing of our situation, that so many are interested in our well-being, and on and on." She leaned forward. "I would imagine that thanks to Kate, we will be the most fashionable people at the ball."

Kate's smile grew. "You will. We are wearing styles that will only begin to catch on midway through the season."

"It's amazing how you keep up on all of this." Lucy watched her. "How do you even know?"

"I read the magazines." She shrugged. "I pay attention. And once you've watched for long enough, you do have a sense of what's coming." And she created the expectation this time. With her fashion plates. It was remarkable, really. She couldn't wait to see if others really did follow her fashion suggestions in *Whims and Fancies.*

"And you have such a good eye. The dresses you chose, the fabric and colors. We will look better than we ever have." Lucy's compliment glowed inside Kate like a happy fire.

"And June, too. She is the most beautiful bride." Grace clasped her hands together.

"Remember all the pieces and adjust your hair for tonight. I just want tonight to be a new beginning for us. The Sisters of Sussex are no longer someone's poor relations. We are a force all by ourselves."

Charity reached for her hand across the carriage. "Thank you, Kate. I think you are correct. After tonight, we will be respected. We have to be."

"Just by looking at the guest list alone." Lucy nodded. "This is the event of the year. Everyone has come to Brighton."

"I'm just happy I get to go." Grace grinned. "And that none

of you are thinking about getting married anytime soon." She looked from sister to sister. "Are you?"

"I'm certainly not." Charity adjusted her skirts.

"I don't have anyone even aware I exist right now." Kate thought of Lord Dennison's incredibly rude comment. "And no prospects."

"I just don't know." Lucy clasped and unclasped her hands.

"Perfect. See? No one is getting married anytime soon." Grace swung her feet.

The carriage pulled in front of their home.

"I love this castle." Grace skipped inside. "I'm going to the kitchen for a luncheon."

"We could ask them to bring us food out to the dining room"

She shrugged. "Who needs that?" She skipped faster.

"Remember to start getting ready with three hours to spare. These things always take longer than we think they will."

Everyone seemed to hear and moved off in opposite directions. Kate was left to herself. So she headed for the library and her drawing materials.

They had found a priceless group of trunks and crates full of books in an unused, broken-down section of the house. June and Morley had immediately created a library, and now, it was one of Kate's favorite rooms. She kept her magazines in there and had designated a desk and portion of the room to her drawing.

She would send a report of the wedding as her written piece to *Whims and Fancies*. She already knew what she would say, which dresses she would mention, and how she would describe June's dress. She'd designed it. But now, she wanted to draw Lord Dennison. Her hurt returned the minute she thought about him. But she tried to put aside her emotion and consider what *Whims and Fancies* would most want to see. His cravat was a statement if nothing else, and she knew it would be of interest to the *Whims and Fancies* readers. As soon as she started drawing his jawline, his jacket, and then worked on the cravat itself, she became lost to her work. It took several attempts and much concentration, but eventually, she got the cravat more or less as he'd worn it.

Amelia's soft voice in the doorway made Kate smile.

"Do I see some drawing going on?"

"Come and see. I'd love your input here." Kate had seen Amelia's work. Her Grace was exceptional at capturing faces.

"Oh, these are good. Kate, I feel like I am seeing it right in front of me. Did he really have a knot that large?" Amelia studied the paper closer. "That's a rather remarkable feat."

"I thought so, too. Overdone, honestly. It detracted from . . ." She cleared her throat. "His other features."

Amelia laughed. "Other features? I noticed the drawing cut off. I can't tell if he is young or old."

Kate pulled out another paper and started roughly drawing him from the hair down. Remarkably, she recreated very specific details about the rise of his hair, the specific waves across, and his nose. It was easy to sketch his nose and mouth. She paused at his eyes.

"Eyes are difficult unless you imagine their expression. That usually helps me," Amelia said.

Kate nodded, biting her lip in concentration. She pictured him as she had last seen him, looking over her shoulder when the sisters had left their pew to walk out of the church. She frowned. He had just insulted her, and his look of contempt was clear in her mind.

As she got closer to finishing, Amelia clucked her tongue. "So he isn't the nicest man you've ever met?"

Kate paused and held the drawing out to see the whole picture. Then she shook her head. "He said something unkind.

And this is the last view I had of him." She shook her head again. "I don't like to see him like this. It brings back the moment too clearly." She almost tossed the paper, but Amelia reached for it.

"I understand the desire to toss it to the fire, but this is incredible. So real. Tell me. What did he say?"

"Nothing I want to think about again. He is just as you see there, contemptuous of others, displeased, and highly judgmental of me."

"Of you?"

"Yes. He . . . he is of the opinion that I am . . . well, apparently, I'm just like every other woman here, care nothing for anyone but myself, wrapped up in my own presentation, with probably naught but straw in my head."

Amelia's gasp was gratifying. "Does he know you heard him?"

"I don't think so, but no matter. It is better I know his real feelings."

"Why? Were you hoping to know him?"

"I . . . was interested in talking to him. He's a paragon of fashion, and I've been intrigued by the things written of him."

Amelia nodded, watching her a bit too closely.

"But, besides a bit of hurt pride, I cannot be affected too deeply. I don't know him at all."

"Hmm. Well, I have now decided we must never like him. Anyone who thinks such things about you does not know you, and if he is so willing to form such a negative opinion without knowing you properly, then . . ." Amelia tsked. "He is not worth our time."

"Precisely. I just need to get his cravat down and whatever garish jacket he will wear this evening. That is all I care to see in him."

"The gown you designed for me is the most amazing I've ever owned."

"Oh, I'm so glad. The modiste was impressed with my suggestions. I was glad for the opportunity to have some influence." Kate had thought it one of the most fulfilling and entertaining moments of her life to lock herself up with the modiste and drawings and material and help design each of the dresses.

And it was worth it. When the sisters all arrived together into the great assembly hall of Brighton, Kate knew the night was going to be a success. Lord Dennison stopped mid-stride, mid-sentence to openly stare at their group. And Kate knew that moment alone would stay in her memory for weeks on end.

But then, he began to walk in their direction. "Oh no, oh no."

Her sisters turned to her. "What is wrong?" Charity stepped in the line of sight between her and Lord Dennison.

"Nothing. I . . . I'm going to hide."

Chapter Three

✿

L ogan moved toward the Standish sisters without even meaning to. Whoever he had just been talking to was so far back in his brain, he didn't bother to try and smooth over his abrupt departure from them.

The sisters stood together in a clump of beautiful gowns and stunning hair, the style he knew the other women in the room would imitate for months on end. And they seemed to be utterly unaware of the effect they were having on the room, and certainly on him. For though the lovely one he'd insulted had certainly seen him, she was no longer even in his sight. The women had circled together in an impenetrable mass.

He told himself he was seeking her out to apologize, to make right his horrifying comment. A disgruntled, hurt reaction meant to be spoken under his breath had reached an innocent woman who no sooner deserved the repercussions of Olivia's rejection than a dove. And she reminded him of just such a bird, come to think of it. But he had no inkling how to make right his supremely rude comment without perhaps further hurting her feelings. For how much of his words had she heard? And how to bring up such a conversation? And truth being, he was being honest, however brutally so. A woman so consumed by the intricacies of fashion could have no other meritable pursuits. He knew, for he'd been in that exact situation for over a year now.

But Logan's movement in their direction had little to do with his need to apologize. He was drawn to them like he had been to no one else. His feet moved of their own volition.

He knew he should not attempt any conversation with her until he'd figured out his manner of apology, but his feet simply did not obey.

But she seemed to have disappeared.

The sisters moved apart, and she was nowhere to be found. The others stepped out into the ballroom, not a single one paying him any mind, and he was left standing alone near the entrance to the room.

Julia stepped to his side. "You were rude just now, walking away in the middle of the duchess's story."

"Was that the duchess?"

Her eyebrow rose.

"Certainly, I know it was the duchess now that you mention it, but at the time . . ." His voice trailed off.

"You need an introduction."

"Pardon?"

"An introduction . . . if you wish to meet Miss Kate."

"Is that her name?" Kate rolled around in his mind, a soft sort of pleasing impression.

The emcee announced, "The bride and groom. Lord and Lady Morley."

Everyone in the room clapped.

Logan tried not to frown at how incredibly, sickeningly happy they looked.

"It's not healthy, you know," Julia said.

"What's not?"

"To feel so many things at once."

"How can you know what I'm feeling? I'm merely proud of my slippers, and not a soul has yet mentioned them." He stepped forward, just enough that his pink, green, and blue slippers with the pointy ends would be in his line of sight.

Lord Tanner approached. "Dennison."

"Tanner."

"I just barely caught up with your cravat from last month."

Lord Tanner lifted his chin.

"My compliments. It is masterfully tied."

"Thank you." He eyed Logan's. "That one seems almost impossible. It's ingenious."

"It took Wiggins weeks to master and two hours to tie."

Julia cleared her throat.

"Oh, excuse me." Lord Tanner bowed to his sister. "Lady Julia, would you like to dance?"

"Yes, I'd love to." She put her hand on Lord Tanner's arm and said to Logan, "Just maybe think before you do anything."

He shook his head. Why were they once again reverting back to their childhood days, where she knew everything and told him what to do?

Emotions all awry, he tried to regain his control over the room, or himself, or something. Off-kilter, he went in search of someone who would appreciate his new slippers.

He made a quick work of the room with his gaze and then grinned. As expected, in a happy group in the corner, standing out as the brightest, most colorful in the room, were just the men he was looking for.

His steps dragged for a moment as he wondered where Miss Kate had gone, but he forced the forward motion and was soon standing in front of the most dandified men at the party. He posed, standing with one foot forward, waiting. Any moment now. He smiled, anticipating their response.

"Lord Dennison?" Her Grace, the Duchess of Granbury approached.

He turned from the others and bowed. "Your Grace. How are you this evening?"

She always dressed simply. But with much class and charm.

"I am well. I couldn't help but notice your singularly gorgeous slippers."

He grinned. "Did you notice? I almost didn't wear them, but then after the wedding today, I knew that the ball would most definitely be a fantastically outstanding slipper occasion."

"I can see why a wedding would do that to a person."

Logan started to laugh, but saw that she was serious, and so he just nodded, feeling uncomfortable with a sudden and sincere conversation.

"I wonder, might I introduce you to the Standish sisters?"

His mind spun with every possible option he could fathom as to why he could not be introduced just then, but nothing would suffice. "Certainly. It would be my pleasure."

"Come." She put her hand on his arm. "Any one of them would be a delightful dance partner . . . and not step on your slippers." Her smile made her all the lovelier.

"I see we are of one mind regarding my slippers." His eyes darted back to his friends, who had just now noticed him, and then returned to their front, where they approached a small group of the sisters.

The duchess curtseyed to them, and he bowed. She placed her other hand on his arm to join the first. "My lovely friends. Might I introduce Lord Dennison to you? Miss Charity, Miss Lucy, Miss Kate, and Miss Grace, and of course, you saw their beautiful sister, Lady Morley, as she was married just this morning."

He took the offered hand from Miss Charity and bowed over it. "I'm delighted to make your acquaintance."

Miss Charity eyed him, as if to ask, "Are you really?" But she only smiled the most demure smile he'd seen on a debutante and nodded. "This is a special day for our family. Thank you for celebrating with us."

"My pleasure. And now I wonder, do you all have free sets to dance? Might one lord dance with each of you?"

They curtseyed. Miss Kate looked away.

"Miss . . . Kate is it?"

Her head snapped back to look at him so quickly, her eyes so challenging, he almost stepped away. "If yours might be the first?" He bowed to hide his own fear of this woman he'd insulted.

Get it together, man.

When Logan lifted his head again and held out his hand, he'd regained something of his usual temperate demeanor. His mouth curled up in his laziest smile, and he waited.

The battle of emotion was much more obvious on her face than he hoped was visible on his own, but she mastered herself in a relatively short space and nodded, placing her hand in his own.

The music for a waltz started, and he almost laughed at her small groan.

"Am I that abhorrent? Or is it the waltz you don't care for? Have you had much opportunity to learn it?"

"I have been sufficiently instructed." Her small chin, raised in defiance to him, charmed him more than intimidated. Somehow, knowing her lovely, small frame would be in his arms helped him feel more in control of his emotions.

"Pleased I am to hear it."

As she moved, a small tinkling sound intrigued him. They stood facing one another. Before he placed his hand at the small of her back, moving in closer for an almost embrace with a woman who had good reason to hate him, he wanted to say something to put her at ease. "Your sister was the loveliest bride I've ever seen. I'm so happy for them both. I'm sure Lord Morley will be blessed his life through."

A spark in Miss Kate's eyes softened as she nodded. "Yes, I believe they are the happiest couple I've yet seen."

He stepped closer.

Her soft intake of breath washed through him as the raging rapids on the river behind his estate, tumbling over rocks and disturbing his peaceful state. Was she affected by him?

His arms ached to pull her closer. But he distracted himself by studying the glorious hair design just below his chin. Her brown curls rose up in a tower and cascaded down around the top of her head.

They moved about the room in quiet, Logan considering the best manner to go about correcting his insulting words.

She said nothing for so long, he wondered if all conversation would be left to him. Then she lifted her chin, her warm brown eyes sparkling at him. "Tell me about your fabulous slippers."

He couldn't have been more surprised. Or more reluctant to talk about something so off subject as his slippers. This was not creating the easy in that he might have hoped.

But he would always lean on his presentation as a manner in which to strengthen his resolve. "Did you notice? I'm quite proud of them."

"How could I miss them? You are the only man in the room to have pink and blue slippers with pointed toes."

He laughed. "I suppose that is so. Although . . ." He winked. "I suspect others might be seen wearing them at a later date."

"I suspect you might be right." She made a pretense of deep thought, and he wondered what she was about. "As clever as they are, I wonder if you've noticed a missed . . . opportunity?"

He frowned. "Missed opportunity? In my slippers?"

"Certainly." She looked down toward her feet, and her slippers poked out for a moment as they moved. A tinkling sound carried up.

"Yours have bells."

She nodded, aware of her triumph.

"Another touch we might see on many a slipper moving forward," Logan said.

"I suspect you are correct," Miss Kate replied.

He studied her. "You're a fashion paragon. Do you . . . Do you dress as you do on purpose?" Could she be like himself, distracting his greater sorrows by becoming a master at disguise? Before he could fall at her feet in hopeful questions, he reminded himself that it was more likely she simply enjoyed fashion, had an eye for it.

"I make a study of fashion, yes, and I enjoy the result." She dipped her head. "Perhaps some would consider it frivolous or . . . unimportant." She looked away, but not before a subtle, soft quiver of her lip caused his heart to clench in guilt.

"The study of fashion has a most important place in our society. I myself spend hours at a time mastering the more subtle arts."

"Your cravat for instance."

"Yes." He eyed her. "This knot is a result of weeks of careful imagining and practice of my valet. Once mastered, it takes two hours to create." As he said the words, by rote, he recognized the superficiality of his words, and for the first time in over a year, he wanted to be real. "In truth, the study of fashion aids me in my effort to endure social events such as this one."

Miss Kate stiffened.

"Perhaps if you were in more elevated company? I know we don't boast as varied a crowd as say, London, but you are among those most notably ranked higher than you. Surely, you can see we are not so far beneath you."

"Not at all. I am making a bumble of my words. The truth of the matter is, I asked you to dance so that I might apologize."

She looked about ready to bolt, so he spoke quickly.

"I know some might call our particular hobby, our interest in fashion as . . . empty-headed and signifying a baser under-standing."

Her eyebrows raised. "Some would?"

"I myself have been known to say such things even while in the very act of emulating a fashion-conscious behavior."

"Hmm."

"But the truth is, I would never want those words to be overheard. A private conversation with my sister is meant to be just that. And were my words spoken in reaction to something else entirely to be overhead, the listener might arrive at the most incorrect assumption of my regard."

"Your . . . regard?"

Logan mumbled around in his mind. Regard. Why had he said regard? "My . . . esteem?" He cleared his throat. Their time together would be ending soon. "For I have the highest respect for your own style choices. Your hair is the most fantastic I've seen. Your dress, the lining at your neck, equally clever and enticing. Your whole manner of presentation is the result of great study, and while I'm unsure why you spend so much effort on these pursuits, they are hardly any to be ashamed of. I know many a person who engages himself in more ridiculous notions." He was thinking primarily of himself. Though he had his own reasons.

There, he'd apologized. Hopefully, she could start to feel less hurt by his words, and he could move on to cards with his friends, in another room.

But she didn't say anything for several measures of their music. When at last she raised her chin again so that he might see into her face, she presented a mask he could no longer read. "You do know your jacket cut is falling out of mode," she said.

He stood taller. "Pardon me?"

"For someone who claims to make a study of fashion, surely you have noticed, the cut of your jacket, it's so last week."

The music ended. Miss Kate curtseyed and turned from him to make her way back to her sisters. Logan followed after her softly tinkling slippers and considered her words. Last week? He resisted looking at his own jacket to be sure of its cut. He knew it well enough. And it was most definitely not last week's fashion. Though he hadn't given thought to the cut of his jacket. Were not all jackets made the same? But what if he were to adjust the cut? Think of the havoc he would wreak on all unsuspecting lords as they scrambled to make their cuts match. His grin started slow and grew before he remembered that his lovely dance partner had just insulted him and was walking away in a small version of a huff, back toward her family.

Well, his apology might not have been accepted, but at least he'd apologized. Now to see if the other sisters would care to dance. Miss Kate's refusal to give him any further attention as he approached rankled somewhat, even though he told himself he didn't care one more whit about her.

Chapter Four

Kate couldn't believe Lord Dennison's audacity. To bring up again his rude comments, to accuse her of eavesdropping. Well, she would not give him the satisfaction of knowing she'd even heard his ridiculous, hypocritical comments. No. Her mind raced to think what she could draw next, that would push the boundaries of fashion even further. Ridiculous, indeed. Not so ridiculous when others read her and followed her suggestions. She'd show him just how un-frivolous her focus on fashion would be.

How unfair to be judged so. When her initial aim was to support her family and keep food on their table? What was his purpose in being utterly fashion ridiculous?

Of all the empty-headed, superficial activities for any lord. Could he not focus more on his voting in the House of Lords? On his tenants? On any such thing? She knew she was sounding quite like him in her own judgment. But to be spoken of in so poor a manner as he had by one who behaved in the same manner still rankled, and greatly so. Was she bound to forgive his weak and accusatory apology? Not anytime soon.

The evening passed in a pleasant enough manner. Kate danced more sets than she ever had. And heard more times than she could count that people would be coming calling. Which she encouraged every chance she could. A study of their clothing choices, particularly the extra accoutrements, was important to her right now. What did they carry with them? And how could she write about such things for *Whims and Fancies*?

The last of the guests were preparing to leave, and June and Morley stood at the door, embracing each of Kate's sisters. She held back a moment with great satisfaction, studying each dress, each fold of fabric, the colors, and June's dress. A masterpiece.

"If only Morley had taken as much care as you sisters have." His voice rolled through her in an irritated pleasure that annoyed her further.

"I imagine he has better things to do than overly concern himself with his appearance."

"Obviously." Lord Dennison's lazy expression hid a wit she guessed was as sharp as the lines of his jacket, which she greatly appreciated. She had only taken a jab at him because she could think of nothing else.

"I think he is a nice foil against the bright and forward-thinking dresses."

"I admit to admiring that image. They make a perfectly pleasing painting."

She would not forgive him for speaking her very thoughts out loud and approached her sisters without another glance in his direction. They all came together in a grand embrace, Morley's arms around her back, the closeness filling her with strength. "Have an incredible trip," Kate said.

"We will. And we shall miss you all terribly." June's eyes welled.

"Oh, no. No tears. We shall be splendid. And the last of the castle renovations just might be complete."

"The last?" Morley shook his head. "Oh no. We have even greater plans for that imitable castle."

Grace giggled. "I'm pleased to hear it."

They separated and moved to the door, where each sister raised a handkerchief in the air as the carriage moved away.

Theirs pulled up next.

She felt Dennison's eyes on her, and she refused to acknowledge him.

"Goodbye, Lord Dennison! Thank you for our dance," Grace called back over her shoulder. "He's watching you." Her smaller murmur in Kate's ear brought her hairs on end in a warm, inviting gooseflesh like she'd never experienced.

"I know."

"Why don't you bid him farewell?"

"Because he is the most pompous, arrogant, self-centered man of my acquaintance." She climbed in after her sisters.

"Well, then." Grace smiled.

Kate didn't expect Grace would smile were she to hear what he had said about her, and the weak and accusing apology. But Kate didn't dare repeat his words. They were painfully, fearfully true, she suspected, and to see for a moment in her sisters' eyes their own agreement would be too much.

Her mind turned instead to her drawings and her plans for *Her Lady's Whims and Fancies*. A delicious plot of revenge tried to niggle its way into her plans. She pushed it aside. She would not stoop. As her fingers toyed with the ribbons on her dress, she considered. But she could discuss Lord Dennison, not by name or course. Because his fashion choices would be the most talked about of the month. Her own personal feelings aside, he was important to their readership.

Sleep came easily even though the castle felt strangely

bereft without June's presence. The next morning found Kate in the library with a tray for breakfast, looking over her sketches. Pleased with the results of her hours of work this morning, she rose and stretched. One last sip of her tea, though cold, and Kate was ready for the day's callers. These visitors would no doubt give her more information to use in next month's *Whims and Fancies*. Because of the lateness of the hour after the ball, she was not expecting anyone until later in the afternoon, so she made her way through the castle.

She loved to go to the as yet unfinished parts to drink in the history of the place. They had found jewels and necklaces from William the Conqueror to his descendants. And every one of them wondered just how they fit into that particular family line. Kate smiled, thinking of dear Morley's wedding gift. What a perfect present, and it had looked so well on June at the ball.

As Kate walked, the walls grew more crumbly and faded, the stone older, the smell more ancient. That was the only way to describe it. Old. And Kate loved every bit of it. Had her family lived in this castle? Had they built it originally? What ancestors called to her from these walls? As her fingers ran along the stone, she moved to the section of walls that had most recently been closed off. She passed them and found her way into some of the older rooms in the house. Grace spent large amounts of time in this part of the castle. Her younger, adventurous self was drawn to it. They had yet to explore old trunks and crates. And they had not yet looked through the old furniture, either.

Kate often found treasures in these rooms. The desk she used for her drawings had been in one of these rooms. She stepped into an older, more dusty space. Something about being with so many items that had been around longer than she helped her put life in perspective. Was there something in these rooms that would help her know more about herself? Just breathing the musty air seemed to strengthen her center. The back corner was filled with furniture, covered in white. But it was the other corner that drew her attention. Old crates they'd only just begun to explore stacked high to the ceiling. June's book treasures were slowly beginning to fill their library. And Kate had seen something that drew her eye last time, something she wanted to explore.

Dresses.

The particular crates she had expressed interest in had been opened for her. Bless their servants. She would never discount the great gift it was to have servants.

As she lifted the first gown, wrapped in linen, she held her breath. Judging by the fabric, it was old, very old. A sense of awe surrounded her as she considered the last person to wear it, the hands that had carefully tucked it away. Her fingers gently feathered over the front of the ancient silk, the embroidery still intact, the greens and browns fascinating to Kate. Colors no one wore now. How interesting. What determined fashion and style? If it were anything like the ton now, the slightest whim written on a fashion plate or worn by someone of significance was enough to send the wealthiest among them seeking out similar styles.

This crate and perhaps others were a treasure. Kate would be back to look through every single garment. But now, she knew their callers would start arriving, and she must prepare herself and alert the others.

After much cajoling to drag Charity from her bed and to convince the others of the importance of imminent guests, four Standish sisters sat in their front receiving room, with tea at their fingertips.

"I should have liked some of cook's eggs," Grace moaned. "Am I to subsist on cakes and tea?"

"If you'd arisen earlier, you could have eaten any number of things." Kate rested a hand on her younger sister's. "But we were up so awfully late. I quite understand."

"We can't be here for too long at any rate. How many are going to come call, really?" Lucy sat precisely upright—the only indication she was anything other than perfectly composed was the tapping of her toes.

Right on the dot, at the awfully dull hour of three in the afternoon, Butler Gibbons announced their first caller. "A Lord Dennison to see you."

Kate gasped before she could stop herself. And the others all turned to her in different reactions of surprise.

"What? I didn't think he'd come." Kate adjusted her skirts that were already perfectly situated and then stood with her sisters.

They all curtseyed in unison.

Lord Dennison entered with a flair. His shoes were more sensible. The hessians tall and reflective in their shine. His cravat what Kate would consider the paragon of afternoon calling cravats, a simple Oriental. His breeches fit to perfection. And his jacket. She laughed to herself. His yellow jacket with beautiful purple and jade embroidery was something to behold.

His ready smile and much more jovial nature made him all the more appealing. All of which Kate tried to ignore.

"And Lord Ballustrade."

Her gaze shot up to the man who stepped in at Lord Dennison's side. He bowed with a double circle of his hands, his head nearly touching his knees, then arose.

One of the most celebrated male fashion experts of their day. This visit would be intensely interesting after all, especially if she could all but ignore the handsome Lord Dennison.

Surprisingly, Lord Ballustrade was dressed in black. A white cravat, simply tied, adorned his neck. She looked twice to be sure nothing extra adorned his breeches or boots or anything.

Surprised at such a simple outfit, she settled back into what she expected—a normal visiting hour. But when he arose and turned so that his vest became more visible, she widened her eyes at the brightly colored band across his middle. She craned her neck to get a better look. Charity nudged her, and she righted herself.

Lord Dennison's eyebrow rose in amusement.

The sisters arose from their curtseys, and then Charity indicated the empty seats. "Please join us for tea. We're so happy you have come."

Lord Ballustrade made his way to the opposite side of their seating, much to Kate's frustration. She couldn't speak to him as an aside very comfortably, but she could look at him, and that would help with her drawings. And then, while she was attempting to get a good look at the man's hessians, Lord Dennison sat at her side.

"Perhaps I have made amends?"

When she turned to him, his face was so close, she moved back a touch, but not before all the flecks of light, the yellows and light blues in his eyes, sparkled at her.

"Amends?"

"Certainly. I have brought the paragon of fashion, the expert himself, to your receiving room. Surely, that amends something?" His tone was light, but his voice held a quality to it that made her search his eyes once more. The varying color once again fascinating her observant gaze.

"I am . . . I'll be honest . . . quite intrigued." Her gaze moved once again to Lord Ballustrade.

"Ask me."

"Pardon?"

"Ask me what you would ask him. I am certain to know what he would say."

She hesitated.

JEN GEIGLE JOHNSON

"His vest is hand-embroidered by his tailor," Lord Dennison continued.

She nodded. "I guessed as much."

"He will be touting a whole series of these new vests through the rest of the season. His launch of the idea is to be this week in Brighton. Your home is the first we've been."

Kate's eyes widened. "We are the very first." She looked from Lord Ballustrade, who was deep in conversation with Lucy, and back to Lord Dennison.

"You are."

She itched to take out her papers. "And will he . . . will he always wear black?"

"Oh no. He has different jacket colors for the occasions, and wildly varied vests as well. But I will draw your attention to the buttons." He leaned forward and squinted.

So she followed suit. "I cannot see the buttons."

"Precisely."

She sat back and frowned.

"They are so tiny as to be unnoticeable. Because . . ."

Lord Ballustrade called over to them. "I see you squinting and talking about me as if I'm not present. What is it? Out with it, man."

Kate laughed. "Oh dear, no."

"She is fascinated by your new vest."

His face lit in pleasure. "Ah, someone who appreciates fashion! Well, upon my word, I am more than happy to discuss everything to do with this vest."

"Perhaps you could promenade?" Lord Dennison lifted his hand.

"Oh, yes, or come closer," Kate said. "I'm most fascinated with your buttons."

"His buttons?" Charity looked like she might turn away completely, but she sat back and watched, nonetheless.

34

"Oh, my dear. You might think something so insignificant as a button would not matter, but let me tell you, the buttons are what make this vest what it is." He stood and moved close enough that he midriff was a mere inches from Kate's nose. "Can you see them?"

She shook her head, glancing at Lord Dennison, who was attempting to keep a laugh at bay. "I cannot see even one button."

"And that is the magic of this vest. See the swirls, the patterns in the embroidery? They are seamless appearing—they go from one side of the vest to the other as if it doesn't even open in the front."

"I see that. It's rather remarkable."

"Too true. I shall pass on your compliments to my tailor. But there are buttons. And they are just so cleverly disguised, you would never know of their presence."

Kate leaned forward, rising to the challenge to discover Lord Ballustrade's buttons, but he turned away, and Lord Dennison leaned back and openly laughed. "You've flummoxed the good Miss Kate. She'll be wondering about your buttons the whole night through."

"As well she should. They will be all the rage in a few weeks' time, and no one but me will be able to create such a work of art." He sat back in his chair and picked up a cake.

"I am quite impressed. Indeed, I've rarely seen anything so fascinating as your hidden buttons," Kate said.

"Rarely? What have you seen that even rivals their ingenuity?"

She cleared her throat and glanced at Lord Dennison. "I was witness to a pair of slippers while dancing that may have come close."

"Oh, she has a point. I, too, saw a pair that not only stood out in color contrast but in sound," Lord Dennison said.

"In sound?" Lord Ballustrade's mouth twitched.

"Yes. Bells. On the tips of the shoes."

He crossed his arms. "And these slippers? They come close to my vest?" He shook his head. "I cannot account for it."

The butler entered again. "A Lady Julia to see you."

They rose, and Kate was immediately taken in by the warm and genuine smile of their newest guest.

"And Her Grace, the Duchess of Granbury."

They remained standing while the room curtseyed anew.

"Oh, Your Grace and Lady Julia, do come in." Charity's tone was all politeness, but Kate knew she would soon pass out from boredom if something more interesting didn't come their way.

Chapter Five

"**A**Lord Tanner, Boxley, and Fenning to see you." They stood again and made room as one of the most opinionated lords in the ton entered the room, eyed Charity, and made a beeline for the chair next to her.

"Oh my," Miss Kate murmured under her breath.

"I think if my sister had not just arrived, I would be on my way to collect Lord Ballustrade and be off," Logan said.

His sister sat at his other side and leaned across. "Miss Kate, is it?" She held out her hand. "I'm so pleased to meet you. I've come today hoping we could have a cozy chat, but it seems this room is full."

Conversation between Miss Charity and Lord Harrison seemed to become quite intense. The other lords who'd come with him watched with amusement. And Logan couldn't say immediately how things would go. "Perhaps a tour? Or a walk on the grounds?" he suggested.

"Oh, the grounds are lovely right now. The weather is gorgeous this morning." Julia said.

"I would love a walk." Miss Kate stood. "For those interested, we are out to the side gardens."

Miss Charity waved to her sister, obviously only half-listening. But Lord Ballustrade and Miss Grace stood immediately.

Lord Tanner seemed interested in a conversation with Miss Lucy, and they gave no indication of having heard anything else in the room. Her Grace stood to join them, but then turned back to the other ladies, looking from one to the other, and sat again.

"Her Grace is a good friend, is she not?" Logan noticed she would stay in the sitting room to help the other sisters.

"One of the best." Miss Kate smiled fondly and waved before they left.

She led them past the front door, seemingly toward a side entrance, just as another carriage arrived. She paused and eyed the equipage for a moment before continuing on.

"Would you like to remain? Will your sisters manage well without the two of you?" Logan paused.

Miss Grace nodded. "They will be fine. The duke will join his wife any moment now, and even Charity will curb her tongue." She laughed. "Oh, perhaps I shouldn't have said such a thing."

"Perhaps not." Miss Kate eyed her, but then linked their arms. "We are happy at least to be out in the fresh air for a time, aren't we?"

"We are."

Logan envied that cozy companionship, and wished for Miss Kate's hand on his arm. But his sister took his other arm instead.

Lord Ballustrade situated himself on the other side of Miss Grace. "I find this smaller group highly enjoyable."

Miss Kate immediately perked up, and Logan wished even more that he had her on his arm instead.

"Tell me, Lord Ballustrade. Tell me more about this lovely vest. The stitches. I can't look away, it is so beautiful."

His friend puffed his chest and began a lengthy discussion of the experience of convincing his tailor to do such a thing.

He murmured, close to Julia. "Do I sound like him when discussing my cravats?" His voice was low, and he knew his sister would respond honestly. He braced himself for her response.

"I thought you *wanted* to appear self-centered and ridiculous."

He cringed. "Thank you, sister."

Her fingers on his arm tugged him closer to her side. "But you are much more charming about it. And more aloof. Except for these last few days, you keep yourself aloof, emotionally distant, unreachable. It . . . adds to the effect." She sighed. "But I don't know why you must behave in this manner. Since you are asking, I will tell you I greatly miss the Logan I've always known."

"Perhaps this was all there ever was to know."

She shook her head. "I cannot believe it. Just like I don't believe Miss Kate focuses so much on fashion simply to amuse herself."

"Does she not?"

"There is an intensity about her interest . . ." His sister's voice trailed off. "I like her."

Logan followed her gaze to the now animated and passionate woman who was discussing thread type and color. "We don't know anything about her."

"And yet, here we are." Julia's knowing gaze prickled at him.

"I'm here simply to make amends. I knew she would like to talk to Lord Ballustrade."

"Hmm."

He knew she didn't believe him. He hardly believed himself.

But why was he here? He certainly had no use for a relationship. He had seen in Olivia what happened when he became close with a woman. "You can erase any thoughts you have about me wanting to pursue a relationship with any simpering, silly woman of the ton. I have no use for their wily ways that reel in and entrap a man, only to leave him alone." The words caught in his throat. The intensity of his feelings created a whisper so forced, it was louder than he anticipated.

Conversation had stopped, and every eye was on him.

Miss Kate's face had become a mask, and the others seemed shocked.

Lord Ballustrade laughed. "I think perhaps Lord Dennison's cravat is too tight."

The others joined in, and Logan frowned. They arrived at a lovely hedge wall with an arbor entrance into something that seemed enchanting, full of roses; the sounds of a fountain trickled out to where they stood.

Another carriage arrived at the front of the castle. And the happy chatter of women reached their ears.

Miss Kate waved, and some of the women headed over to them.

Logan groaned.

"If you are going to be so surly, we should go," Julia said.

"We came separately."

"Then I'll be more precise. You should go. Unless you can behave in a more pleasant manner. No one here needs to be insulted by you."

"I'm not making the best amends, am I?"

"Not in the slightest."

"I cannot help myself. She hurt me." The words fell from his lips like the others had, without his planning them. When he turned to Julia to see their impact, he had to look away from the tears and pity on her face.

He handed her a handkerchief. "Please, sister, you make me feel like a wet, half-drowned puppy with your compassion."

"You are nothing of the kind. But a sister can feel things, can't she?"

"You wouldn't be you if you didn't." He sighed. "And how may I make even greater amends?"

"I'm not sure your plans at making amends are working in your favor."

"Too true."

Miss Kate was now walking on Lord Ballustrade's arm, entering the gardens alone.

"Perhaps it is for the best," Logan said. "If they make something of themselves, she just might think of me as the cause, and then my amends will be complete."

"I suspect you might not be satisfied with such a result." Julia tugged at him to follow the couple. "But I will stop speaking. You will lash out again and pit yourself against those whom we hope to befriend."

He reluctantly allowed her soft tug on his arm to lead him into the gardens. Miss Grace waited for a group of women who were chattering and laughing. She seemed to know them and had stepped in their direction.

"I'm going to distract Lord Ballustrade. You walk with Miss Kate and use your best manners."

"What? No."

Julia stepped away, and he had no choice but to follow. They both approached a singularly stunning cascade of roses to hear Miss Kate say, "There is just no imitating such a glorious display. Nothing in art, no clothing, nothing I've read can equal this masterpiece right here." The expression she lifted up into the sun as she gazed upon the flowers had such a serenity, such a peace of mind that Logan wanted to step closer. Did peace rub off on a person?

He reached out a hand to brush against the soft petals of a low-hanging rose. Then cupped it carefully so that he might smell it. "We could never imitate such beauty, no, but at times, I see this glorious demonstration reflected in others."

Miss Kate's eyes lit with interest. "What an intriguing thought. Not an imitation, no, but a reflection, shining back what beauty is possible from the limited reflection."

Logan watched her face with some unveiled fascination as she considered his words. And then, without thinking, he held out his arm. "Could we continue this conversation while we circle the gardens?"

"And I would love some time with Lord Ballustrade." Julia linked her arm with his. "Perhaps I can finagle his next fashion plans and be the first to know."

Miss Kate looked wistful for a moment until Logan murmured, "I can tell you his plans."

Then she turned the full attention of her large and attentive eyes and full mouth on him. He had not yet studied her mouth, but now that he had looked, he couldn't look away. But he must.

When his gaze returned to her eyes, he grinned at her raised brow. Then he started their walk along the edge of the gardens.

She surprised him by starting the conversation. "I admit to being quite struck by your comment and have now determined to attempt my own reflection of all the beauty I see."

"I admit to thinking of you when I said those words."

She stumbled. "You . . . were?"

"Certainly. Your face just now, staring up into the flowers, was a reflection of their beauty, your own peace." Why was he being so open and baring his soul to this woman? "I thought it lovely."

She nodded. "Thank you."

They walked in silence a moment more. And he knew this

was his chance to make all right between them. "I do apologize for my harsh words. You were not meant to hear them, and in truth, they weren't directed at you."

"I think I understand. You are hurting. And something particularly difficult came to mind, so you lashed out, not thinking any would hear but your sister?"

"Yes, more or less that."

"And don't you think your sister might also not wish to hear such a thing? Who wants to hear such negativity, whether directed at your own person or not?"

"No one. Surely. I understand what you are saying. I'm merely apologizing for the manner in which my words affected you."

"I see. You know, you don't know me at all. You have no idea why I do what I do, and what if fashion were my passion? What is wrong with a passion when so many of our acquaintance have none? Better to be passionate about something than endlessly bored or critical about everything."

"Yes, point taken. As I said, I'm here to apologize about the one time . . ."

"I will accept your apology, but I cannot help but think you will be dreadful company until you find a way to once again be happy with your situation. To appreciate others for the things they most enjoy, to allow them . . . space. You know, I first decided to make a study of fashion out of necessity? And it has become a passion. You wouldn't know because you made an immediate and rash judgement of me, one that was unmerited, undeserved."

Logan kept his frustration below the surface. No need to insult the woman again in the act of apologizing, but Miss Kate was not making things easy. "And as I said, I'm sorry for my words—my unthinking words, spoken in anger, were directed at another, but you bore the brunt." There. Now perhaps, she would leave it be.

"Is that why you've come? To apologize?"

"Yes. I made a bumbling mess of my apology at the ball, and have come to further rectify my unthinking words."

"Then I thank you." She stepped nearer. "Not many have the courage or humility to do such a thing. I'm happily surprised to see that you do."

Surprised? Irritation brewed. But he wouldn't respond. Of course, she might be surprised. He'd given precious few people any reason to think he was a person of any depth. Was she not making assumptions about him?

"Thank you," he said. He gritted his teeth and tried to pay closer attention to the lovely garden. "Your gardeners are excellent."

"Oh, thank you. Lord Morley has done so much to make this place the beauty it once was. He and the Duke of Granbury are a godsend to us."

"I see that. I would enjoy a tour of the castle. I'm quite fascinated by the history."

"There is an old crate I think you might enjoy. It was filled with gowns."

He snorted.

And she frowned.

"I agree. I would enjoy something so intriguing. Perhaps I might enjoy it more were it to have the latest styles of jackets in our day and time. Did you not mention that mine was out of date?"

Miss Kate's skin colored a pretty pink, and Logan enjoyed the view for a moment.

"I did say that—however, I was merely doing my own version of lashing out at you. Your jacket is just lovely today. I think if you were to stand next to these next roses up here, you would match perfectly."

Was she making fun, or was she complimenting him? He couldn't tell, but he stepped up to the roses, put a hand in one pocket, and lifted his chin, as though posing for a portrait.

Lord Ballustrade called over to him, "Oh, where is the painter when we need him?"

But Miss Kate laughed, and that made all the antics worth it. Her face lit with her happiness. "You do match. That lavender and especially the green look they belong right here in our garden."

"Then I shall have to return. And you know what you've done."

"What is that?"

He returned to offer his arm again.

Her returning hand comforted with the feeling that he had missed in its absence.

"I shall not be able to wear this particular jacket or these colors without thinking of you."

"That is a quandary."

"Why a quandary?"

"Because if I come to mind at every use of these bright colors, I will be on your mind much indeed."

Logan considered her words, then turned to catch her eye. "And now I'm wondering if that would be such a quandary at all."

She didn't respond, but her small smile in response gave him a strange sort of hope. Was he hoping for more with the lovely Miss Kate? He hadn't thought so.

"And now, we shall enter the final gardens to see the lovely fountain."

"I've been hearing its delightful sounds through the whole

of our conversations. And I would think only at how much I missed seeing it in person were we to turn back now."

The fountain was simple in many ways. It didn't rise up to the sky like some. Nor did it boast multiple sea creatures or mer-people, like he'd seen in others. A lone woman stood tall, her face to the sky. She was surrounded by four other women, all in various angles and positions, some pointing outward, some looking down, one looking up into the sky with the first. He was stunned by the beauty in the expression. He moved to stand in front of one. She swished her skirts, her chin was lifted, and she looked to have an energy about her. "This is quite good." He looked to Miss Kate and back at the sculpture. "This is you."

She nodded. "Yes. Lord Morley had this commissioned as soon as June said yes."

He chuckled. "Absolutely a man in love."

"We are all in love with him. He's the brother we have often wished for. He was almost immediately a part of our family, even before June and he were certain they belonged together."

"Belonged together." Logan almost snorted, but wisely kept his cynicism to himself.

"Yes." Miss Kate's expression told him he best not challenge the idea, so he didn't.

"I'm happy for them." There. That should suffice.

"But you do not believe they belong together?" Her arms crossed her chest.

Confound it. Couldn't she just leave well enough alone? He was having a difficult enough time of it, keeping his words placid and unremarkably supportive. "How could I know whether or not they belonged together?"

"Precisely."

"Then I am even more pleased for them."

"But you don't believe in such things."

"I did not say that."

Her frown deepened.

"This frown. That is unfair. As I've said nothing to indicate any sort of disagreement."

"But you are thinking it."

"And how could you know that?" He laughed. Her lips had almost formed a pout, and he was delighted to have elicited such a response. Now that he hoped they were on safer ground, he shrugged. "I once thought such things were possible."

She nodded and said nothing more. Perhaps his answer was sufficient.

"They still could be."

"Hmm. Perhaps for some."

They circled the fountain and joined Julia, who asked, "Can you guess which sister is which?" He reached his hand down to trail in the water.

"Have you found Miss Kate?" Julia continued, grinning.

"Right away."

Lord Ballustrade pointed upward. "Lady Morley, certainly."

"And that must be Charity," Julia said. The figure had her hand out, but as though she were speaking. "I admire her opinions, her well-studied thought." Julia nodded.

They discussed each sister until Miss Grace arrived with the others.

Without thinking much about it, Logan stood taller, his stance changed, his hand went to his hip, and he distanced himself from their group.

Miss Kate eyed him for a moment, but then she went to the others. Their greeting and cheerful carryings on seemed farther away. Julia joined him. "Are you ready to go?"

"Yes, I think all is well now. We can leave this family in peace."

"Can we?" Her one wiggling eyebrow irritated him, but he displayed his most bored expression. "Why would we not?"

Their stroll around the opposite side of the garden and then out the exit was slow and unnoticed, but as his eyes flitted back, Miss Kate's gaze met his own. She nodded, and he left.

And that was the end of his interactions with Miss Kate.

"Thank heavens, that is over with."

Julia smiled some kind of secret that he had no use for, and they made their way to the front and their waiting carriage.

Chapter Six

K ate watched Lord Dennison's retreating form until she could no longer see him. She could no sooner make him out than she had earlier. But she did forgive him somewhat. His words still stung, but he'd attempted with a good heart to apologize, and how could she hang onto bitterness when no hurt was intended?

Even later in the day, while drawing his oversized cravat for *Whims and Fancies*, she had warm thoughts toward him. She hoped he would take her drawings and comments about his style in the spirit they were meant. She supported his difference, his uniqueness of style and fashion-forward sense. She understood it. She wasn't certain why he had become such a paragon of fashion, but she herself appreciated his skill. Even though her words might have poked a bit of fun, she hoped that they would only bring him greater notoriety and attention, which he seemed to crave. She paused. Perhaps not attention. He craved . . . influence? Or power? Or perhaps it was just simply distance.

The sisters met in the family sitting room in the upstairs

area of the house. Amelia and Gerald had joined them with their children. And Kate thought that life could only be better and more complete if June and Morley had already returned.

"Is this not the most perfect group?" Grace kicked her foot lazily at Kate's skirts.

"And what shall we do today?" Charity lifted another sheaf of paper, her pen flying across the page.

"You look as though you are quite distracted already." Kate laughed.

"I am." Charity dipped her quill in ink. She kept writing. "Just considering our afternoon. Shall we go walk the promenade?"

Kate considered. "I think that a lovely idea. While many are still in town, I'd love to go see them all."

"And we might see many of the others . . . Is there a dance at the assembly this week?"

"I think there is one Thursday."

Charity continued her writing.

"Are you working on your novel?"

She shook her head. "This is in response to Lord Harrison. We were never able to come to an agreement, and there are still some things remaining to be said."

"Will you read it to him next you see him?" Grace moved closer to her to look over her shoulder.

"Probably not. But I feel better once the words are out, even if on paper." She studied her words. "Perhaps I would send them somewhere. Who knows, but I could have a bit of space in a paper someday."

Kate shifted in her seat. She had space in the paper. And what did she use it for? She chided herself. She used it to raise money. And she enjoyed her space, no matter what she used it for. "You might make more enemies than friends if you were to be too bold to too many."

Charity paused. "Care I for friend-making? Who needs friends of the wrong variety? Perhaps if I spread my opinions widely enough, I will merely attract those like-minded people who would make a soulmate kind of friend."

"Or husband." Lucy looked disturbed.

"What is it, dear?" Grace moved over to sit by her.

"Nothing, I think."

"Are you enjoying getting to know Lord Kently?" Kate asked.

Charity nodded but said nothing. And Kate could scarce believe her.

"He's everything he should be, isn't he?"

"If you like pompous lords who view themselves supremely above others."

"You just didn't like it that he still doesn't agree with you, no matter how much you try to convince him otherwise."

"That is definitely part of what forms my opinion of him. If a man can't see reason when spoken plainly to his face . . ."

"Do you ever wonder if your extreme opinions and desire to be contrary might prevent your ability to marry?" Kate almost wished to swallow back her words.

Charity shook her head. "No." Then she continued writing.

"I think I shall ring for luncheon right here, and then should we prepare for a promenade on the green this afternoon?" Kate asked.

"Yes!" Grace twirled around the room. "I shall wear my new yellow day dress and bonnet." She moved to Kate and squeezed her across the shoulders. "I'm so happy you have devoted your life to fashion. We have the most lovely dresses I've ever seen on anyone."

Kate smiled. But inside, she wondered at Grace's comment. Devoted her life to fashion. Well, why couldn't she devote her life to fashion? And the stronger question: Had she devoted her life to fashion? She cared about other things. Her family. She'd devoted her life to her family, in truth, and none of them knew it.

And now, her work was not necessary. But she continued. She enjoyed the influence. She enjoyed making women and men beautiful. She enjoyed that she had a bit of space in a paper that people read. That was thrilling to her. Perhaps, one day, she'd use it to say a bit of something more.

Hours later, they exited their carriage out onto the green. The great, round, bulbous towers of the Royal Pavilion rose up in the sky, offering shade to them for a moment.

"The sun is so bright. I am happy we have brought the parasols."Kate squinted up into the sun.

"Yes." Lucy carefully covered her pale skin. With her raven-dark hair and creamy, soft skin, she of them all needed to take great care in the sun.

Charity seemed not to care at all. She had a bonnet, but only because it was more shocking than even she would allow to appear outside at this hour without one.

Lucy raised her hand to indicate a rather large crowd walking about on The Strand. "Goodness. Everyone has come to promenade this afternoon. It looks as though all of our wedding guests have shown up here on the lawn."

"And their friends and family." Kate nodded.

"And I'm drawn more to the sea. Can we begin over there?" Grace pointed away from the pavilion to the edge of the promenade, which led out to the ocean.

"Yes, and can we visit the cliffs again? It's been an age." Lucy's skirts were extra pretty, so much so that Kate was admiring them for the second time. The stitches in the hem were whimsical. The colors were so cheery. Kate wished for a few more just like it.

"I don't think we've been back since the kite-flying and picnic." Charity adjusted her bonnet.

"Too true." Kate shook her head. She'd found it interesting, the clothes women chose to wear on a picnic. And here on the promenade. Bonnets, parasols, and frilly dresses seemed to rule the day. Bright whites, colors in pastels. Nothing dark. And sensible shoes. She smiled.

"What are you grinning about? All the bright colors?" Charity smirked.

"Not at all, actually. I was thinking of Lord Dennison's ridiculous slippers."

"As if yours were any less ridiculous. Did anyone else comment on your bells?" Charity had never shown an ounce of interest in anything Kate wore, not really. But she seemed interested now.

"Not a soul. They were small enough to not be noticed unless attention was drawn to them." Kate wondered what others would think of her drawings in next week's *Whims and Fancies*. She'd included one plate dedicated to Lord Dennison, and the other to herself. But naturally, she didn't draw either of their faces, or name names, just included the fashion choices of each.

Then she'd gone ahead and drawn Lord Ballustrade's vest. Because she knew once she'd described it, *Whims and Fancies* might include it as well. She had only been given space for two before, but they just might increase it to three with so tempting an offer. And that meant more by way of payment.

Even though they seemed to be in good stead, even though Lord Morley had promised to care for them all, she couldn't help but take her own precautions. Kate remembered the moment when her parents had died. Not many of the others knew she still held this memory. But their nurse had come bustling into the school room and nursery. "Gather your things.

Everything you most care about. Heavens only knows what they'll let you take with you."

The scared faces of her sisters, the servants, and her nurse made her reach for one thing: her sweet doll her mother had sewn.

They were hustled out of the home with a single trunk. June had collected what she could of their mother's and father's personal items. All jewels had to stay. Even most of her gowns. But the daughters were allowed some of the more personal items: a portrait miniature, a few books, and her mother's writings.

The cold days in one home or another, displaced more often than solid, then the arrival of their broken-down and drafty cottage had stuck with her. The injustice of such a disruption, the inability of any of them to make a way for themselves. She had vowed to do something, anything, to help her family.

And she continued. Never again would she be at the mercy of the wind. She was building a manner in which to provide for herself, and her sisters.

What if she never married? What if Lord Morley passed on? What if his estate crumbled? There were too many what ifs in the scenario that kept the sisters at the mercy of all others. And Kate knew how quickly life could be taken from someone she loved, and she knew what happened when careful consideration to the after effects were not adhered to. Was she overly concerned with fashion? Perhaps. Had she good reason to be? Yes, most certainly. Did she love it as well? Yes, she did.

She giggled as a pair of women in perfectly matching dresses walked by arm in arm.

"Are they twins?" Grace lifted her chin to point them out.

"I don't know. They certainly look as though they are. Sisters, at the very least," Kate said.

"Why don't you dress us in perfectly matching dresses?" Grace laughed.

"Because she knows we would never agree." Charity crossed her arms. "And I would never be seen wearing dresses that matched precisely. Do we belong in the nursery still?"

"And your styles are so different, I couldn't manage a dress we would all want to match." She nudged Charity. "But a little matching at a wedding would be in order."

"I don't have a style." Grace sighed.

"Oh, you do."

"No. For now, my style is younger sister. You always dress me in something befitting my age."

Kate laughed. "You know, you have a point. Would you like to be officially out?"

"I think that decision must be addressed by June and Morley," Charity said.

"I'm just asking her. I'm by no means about to determine her position in society."

Charity stepped closer. "I know. I'm sorry. I just don't wish for Grace to grow too quickly, nor for any of you to fall in love. One is enough."

"Well, especially since Morley just moved in. If one of you gets married, you'll leave. And maybe far away. And when shall we be together again?" Grace's pout grew.

"You are all too melancholy for me. I wish to think of other things." Lucy swirled her skirts.

"I as well. Did anyone bring a kite?" Charity looked up into the clouds.

"There is close to nothing to do at a promenade. I agree." Kate had studied every bit of a person she could and had found them all dressed the same, with nothing special to report about any of them.

Then trumpets blared.

"Prinny! I didn't know he was in town." Lucy hurried her feet.

"Nor I." Charity frowned.

The doors to the Royal Pavilion opened, and servants in red livery poured out of the entrance like red mice.

"Let's move closer. I'd like to see what is happening." Lucy's eager eyes drank in the scene.

"Yes, let's." Kate linked arms with her sister. In this, they were of one mind. For a firsthand viewing of Prince George's choice of promenade clothing would be good news indeed.

They hurried as fast as they could. As they drew closer, the crowd jostled them, and they found themselves quite hemmed in.

A man stood at Lucy's side. He was young, and shabbily dressed. But a dimple appeared on his cheek as he said to no one in particular, "Well, this is a fine introduction to all my closest neighbors."

Many around him chuckled.

Another grinned. "Didn't expect to embrace a town full of perfect strangers today."

"Not that I mind."

"Some of these strangers are lovely." The first man dipped his hat to Lucy, who looked away, but the slight pink to her cheeks surprised Kate. Had she been truly affected by a man? Then a commotion up ahead drew all their attention. The prince himself stepped out his door. Kate stood on the tips of her toes but only saw a portion of his clothing.

Then a voice behind her made her smile. She tried to turn, but she couldn't manage for the crowd.

"He is wearing deep reds. Odd for this time of year, and hot. But his gold brocade and tassels make him look somewhat like drapes or an upholstered chair."

Kate laughed. "What else? I can't see."

"His slippers are more garish than mine. His hat seems to sit lopsided on his head. It's more a beret than a true hat. His hands are flashing and glinting in the sunlight. I can imagine it to be rings? And his breeches are very tight." Lord Dennison cleared his throat. "I mention it because he looks as though he has eaten much more during his mealtimes than the last time I'd seen him."

"Anything else remarkable? Something we've perhaps not seen him wear before?"

"Isn't that enough? He is wearing drapes and upholstery."

"I suppose." She sighed.

Then his quiet voice continued. "The embroidery on his jacket is of a fox hunt. It is meant to recreate the hunt he went on last season. A flash of red in the forest is the fox that got away. He's determined to catch him next time."

"How can you know this?"

"He told me so himself."

Kate's heart picked up in excitement. "What else?"

"He's gesturing this way."

"What?"

The crowd parted to their front.

Lord Dennison bowed to her and everyone around them, then made his way to the prince. Dennison had worn matching colors, and had retied his new creation in thick folds beneath his chin.

Kate told herself that her heart was racing because of the new plates she could draw and further words to add to another package she mailed to London, but something about Dennison's sudden appearance, the details he must have known she craved, the spark of interest in his eyes as he passed, had something to do with the racing and the fluttering in her stomach.

Chapter Seven

A fter an afternoon with Prince George and all the most fashion-conscious of his set, Logan was ready for something more . . . real. Feelings of unease festered for the next two weeks.

He'd not felt so dissatisfied in many months. Why of all the time in his life did his superior presentation not do anything more for him than momentarily distract? Why did he yearn for more?

The picture of Miss Kate's upturned face returned often to his memory. What was it about her that so intrigued his every thought? And was it her fault he now felt this itch of dissatis-faction? What more was a man to do with his life than to prom-enade with the prince himself? How many men of his acquaintance would spend their lives hoping for just such a moment?

He tried to shake off his feelings, but found himself wondering if there was any way to see Miss Kate again.

Once back to their townhome that sat on the very street of The Strand, he meandered into his sister's drawing room.

She seemed to be hard at work with a needle, poking it in and out of the fabric, her face a vision of supreme concentration. Beautiful.

Logan sat beside her.

"And to what do I owe this great honor?"

He chuckled. "What are you making?" He peered over her shoulder at a charming scene. "Oh, I recognize this. Well done. The copse of trees behind the house on our estate."

"Yes, the very one."

"What will you do with it?"

"I was planning to gift it to Mrs. Wellsley."

He sat back, staring at his sister. "To your governess?"

"Certainly."

"I thought you loathed that woman."

Julia shook her head. "I didn't loathe her. I just resisted anything that required effort on my part. But now I see that all of her proddings were of huge benefit."

"And so you are sending a sort of peace offering?"

"No. I have already thanked her. We are friends. I just know she would appreciate this scene. Did you know she is now older, and lives with her brother and his family?"

"I didn't know." Logan had no idea where his old tutors lived or what they did with their time. Some had been ancient enough when they'd taught him.

Normally, he would be making his way to the card room or to a men's club in Brighton. He might be visiting the stables at the Royal Pavilion, betting on a horse, or planning the next hunt. But again, nothing seemed to hold the same appeal.

But sitting next to his sister watching her do needlepoint did not seem a good substitute, either.

"Perhaps we could attend the library?" he asked.

She paused in her next stitch to look up into his face. "Pardon me?"

"Or a museum? Is there a place to peruse art in Brighton?

"Art? A library?" She rested her hoop in her lap. "Have you looked through our own portrait gallery? Have you read even one of the books in our library here in Brighton?"

"Isn't this the place where Father sent his historical tomes?"

"Yes, the very ones."

He considered her. "Very good. I shall go sit in the library."

Julia said nothing as he left, but soon, the sound of her slippered feet following behind made him smile. "Have you now acquired an interest for the history of warfare in England?" Logan asked.

"I have a new interest in this side of you."

He turned.

She carried her needlepoint.

"Excellent. I'd love some company."

"I as well. I think our aunt would sleep away the day and night if given the choice."

"And so here we are, siblings left to our own devices."

"I remember many such times when this opportunity was not lost on our younger selves."

"We lived for just such a moment." He smiled, a portion of that old, brazen youth rebellion lighting an old, forgotten piece of his heart. "You know what we have never done?"

"What?"

"Sea-bathing."

Julia laughed. "We have sea-bathed."

Logan thought for a moment, and then shook his head. "Doesn't count. We haven't sea-bathed as adults."

"Are you saying you'd like to give it a go?"

He considered her. "I'm saying I'd like to give it a go the way it is supposed to be done."

"Well, for you, I see no difference. You simply strip your shirts and jump into the water. Me, on the other hand . . ." She shook her head. "I surmise that Charity would be willing to go sea-bathing the way we used to. Where a woman could run from the shore into the water without that small, house-like contraption they've created."

"I wonder if we can finagle some method of sea-bathing that wouldn't destroy your precious reputations as well as allow for some diversion."

"If you think of such a thing, I would love to participate."

They opened the door to the library. For a moment, Logan was immediately transported back to his days at Oxford. The smell of old books and paper and bindings tickled his nose. His fingers itched to open the pages like they hadn't in many, many years. His pace picked up as he walked the aisles of his father's surprisingly full library. "Napoleonic papers, even. How do we have those?"

"I think he left instructions to his book sellers to keep updating the library."

"That's incredible of him. Even in death, he was hoping to enrich our lives."

"They were so good to us, our parents."

"Mother still is, in her own way," Logan said.

Julia's soft sigh brought his arm across her small shoulders. "She is lucid now and again. When we return, let's pay her a visit," he suggested.

Her silent nod told him more than any response could.

She wiped at her eyes and then moved to sit in one of the two most comfortable chairs in the room, bringing a lantern and candle close. Soon, she was lost again to her stitching, but there was a serenity about her that spread to Logan. He moved down the next aisle. "And these go back. This bit here shows a history of the area in Sussex."

She didn't respond, and he knew he'd completely lost her interest.

"William the Conqueror? Did you know that the Normans built some of this area? That Standish Castle—that was built by William himself?"

"Hmmm."

He lifted a volume. Did they say they'd inherited the property from a distant cousin? Or the duke had inherited? Logan was immediately intrigued by the history of the place. And he enjoyed the use of his mind. As if he'd dusted off a shelf or two in his memories, old habits of comparing facts and putting things to memory came into play. Before long, he was lost to the puzzle of history.

He and his friends at Oxford had drafted a bill while taking a class on parliamentary procedure and the rule of law in Great Britain. They had all selected Logan as the voice, and then they had debated their bill on a mock floor of the House of Lords. Everyone played a different person. Most chose to play their own family or relations, for those who had them, and Logan had taken on his father's place, but pushed for a bill that was more forward-thinking than his father had ever been. They had researched for weeks on end, the men willing to stay late hours in the library and to argue with and challenge him until the wee hours of the morning. Until when the day finally came to start holding sessions of mock Parliament, he was ready.

The experience had been one of the most thrilling of his life. When all was finished, they'd passed some of the most valuable laws and changes necessary in Great Britain, more so than had been done in years in reality.

And he'd presented it all to his father, as had the other men on his team. He wasn't certain the exact response of every member of the real House of Lords, but his own father had nodded and frowned and said things like, "Interesting . . . oh, how droll."

So much so that Logan had left his office thoroughly

deflated. When he had once thought their idea revolutionary and important, he now felt foolish.

He placed a marker in the current history of William the Conqueror in Sussex and pulled out the next book. When he opened it, a sheaf of papers fells out.

As he opened them, he recognized the very proceedings and minutes from their mock parliamentary experience, including the bills they had written and changes they had put into place.

"Would you look at that." He carried them over and sat in the chair next to his sister. Were his actions trite and naïve? Would they still read with the same importance he'd thought they held so many years ago?

Where were his Oxford friends now? Interestingly, Lord Balllustrade was one. The others were in London, but not present at any of the gambling halls or races, or even at Whites very often. He supposed they might have stepped in to play a stronger role in preparation for their roles in the House of Lords. He had no idea, but thinking of them now made him want to reconnect with old friends. He moved to a desk, still clutching their proceedings in his hand, and pulled out sheaves of paper, a quill, and an inkwell.

By the time he had finished reading his old proceedings and writing each of his old school chums, the candles had nearly burned down, and Julia had left. He pulled a pocket watch out and was stunned at the passage of time.

But he wanted to present himself at the assembly dance that evening. Were any of his Oxford friends here in Brighton? He hadn't given them any thought earlier and had seen none of them.

He rushed up the stairs, passing Julia's opened door. She sat at her dressing table, her maid working a familiar style. "Are you going to do a Standish style?"

"Oh, have we named it? Yes. I am going to make my hair to

look like Charity's did at the church. She sat in front of me, and I spent the entire time studying her pins and the curls."

Logan laughed. "Excellent. I best begin my own preparations."

"Yes, you best. I don't wish to be more than thirty minutes late, mind you."

"I'll be quick about it. A simple cravat, my normal jacket." He paused. "Do I even sound like myself?"

"Yes. You sound exactly like yourself." Her grin filled him with happiness. And then he took off down the hall to find his valet, who was no doubt in a frenzy at the small amount of time they would have to prepare.

Chapter Eight

Kate entered the assembly room with no purpose other than to enjoy herself. She'd seen enough fashion choices to last for weeks of articles and plenty of drawings. She had sent off her drawings from the wedding and ball. And had stacks of ideas for more. Just the appearance of Prinny alone, not to mention the men of his set, could provide any number of fashion plates. She laughed every time she thought of her description of Lord Dennison's cravat. Would the ton know it was him she described? He would surely know. And would he wonder who had seen it to describe it so precisely?

Amelia joined her at her side. Her teal dress with sparkling jewels and stunning overlay made Kate smile. "Do you suppose there is a lord here to catch your eye?" She patted Kate's hand. "Besides for the interest in his manner of dress?"

Kate laughed. "I was just wondering that very thing."

In truth, she was wondering if Dennison would come. What would he wear tonight? She had a particular headdress she was anxious to hear his opinion of. But she didn't want to admit such a thing to Amelia, or herself. Any number of lords could provide equal entertainment and amusement, and she was looking forward to filling her dance card if possible.

The sisters crowded together with Amelia just off the entrance to the assembly room. Everyone seemed in high spirits and particularly lighthearted.

"Grace, try not to be led away by an earl this time." Charity placed an arm across her sister's shoulders. "We could not live without you."

Though lighthearted, every sister felt the anxiety that Grace's plight one night when she had disappeared had caused each one of them.

"Everyone is still here." Lucy's calculating eyes searched the room. "We shall have an excellent evening indeed."

"Especially if all we desire is to entertain ourselves. No other purpose." Kate stood taller. Several lords were looking in their direction, and closer, others were making their way toward them.

"I don't know what else our purpose could be at such an event but to entertain ourselves." Grace's gaze flit to Charity. "Unless you are trying to convince the passage of a new bill in the House of Lords."

Amelia laughed. "Which we can all agree, even the men, is a topic better served in drawing rooms, over card games, and indeed, in the actual House of Lords."

Charity looked about to argue, but four lords approached with the Duke of Granbury, who claimed his wife's hand.

A man with hair the color of the rocky pebble beach bowed over Kate's hand. "Could I interest you in a set?"

"Lord Tipton?" She nodded. "I would love to."

He placed a hand over hers on his arm and led them to the bottom of the line for a country dance. "Miss Kate. How have you been since the wedding?"

"Excellent. I feel like so much has happened, and yet nothing at all."

"And they are off on their trip?"

"Yes. We miss them dreadfully. But I am happy for my sister."

"The castle is so intriguing; I loved our tour. Perhaps I might return for another? Have they completed any more of the rooms?"

"Oh yes. You are welcome anytime." Was he truly interested? Making conversation in a polite manner only? She could never tell. They continued on in much the same manner. And she couldn't help but notice that Lord Dennison was not at the ball.

Until he arrived, toward the end of her set with Lord Tipton. The very air seemed to change, and the gaze she felt on herself could only belong to him. She lifted her lashes as she turned in place and then circled with Lord Tipton.

Lord Dennison stood at the entrance to the room, and his gaze stretched across the room to her.

She finished out the set with Lord Tipton. He led her toward the tables and the lemonade. "Would you like one?" he asked. "I find if I don't remember to wet my lips, I become quite parched by the end of the evening."

"Yes, thank you. I would appreciate a lemonade very much." And the drinks were closer to where Lord Dennison stood, now surrounded by a small crowd of men with other ladies looking on.

As soon as Kate lifted a cup to her lips, Lord Dennison stepped through the group and made his way toward her.

"Don't look now." Lord Tipton smirked. "The venerable Lord Dennison is on the approach."

"Oh?" She raised her eyebrows.

"I've heard his cravat is somewhat ridiculous, but he doesn't appear to be sporting it this evening."

"Ridiculous? I thought it was touted as much revered."

"Ah, you haven't seen the latest *Whims and Fancies*. I have it on good authority—my sister reads every column—that he was quite overdressed. There is a touch, a fine line to playing a complete fop and dressing with precision and style." He stood taller, and Kate wondered if his actual chest size enlarged.

"Yes, I see."

The man spoken of bowed at her front. "Miss Kate." His voice and appreciative tone rippled through her. "Might I have your next dance?"

"Hello, Lord Dennison. It's good to see you again. Certainly." She curtseyed low. Then he left her to her lemonade while the instruments prepared for the next set.

"Thank you, Lord Tipton. Do you know where I might get a copy of the latest *Her Lady's Whims and Fancies?*" Kate asked.

"I think my sister said there are a couple in the ladies' retiring room, or perhaps in the foyer entrance on tables, or the rooms for cards?" He shrugged, then bowed. "Thank you for our set. I'd like to come calling."

"Certainly. Come anytime."

She left him and moved to stand beside Lord Dennison, who waited on the edge of the dance floor. "I hope I didn't pull you away from an important conquest?" His eyebrow twitched, and she wanted to laugh, but his question was too bold.

"I don't know what you are talking about."

"Hmm. I'm sure you don't."

"And what about you? Are you set to conquer any hearts?"

"Me? Not a single one."

She couldn't hide her disappointment. Where was it coming from? Did she want a lord such as Lord Dennison to set out to conquer her heart? Certainly not. Did she?

But then his expression changed, and she held her breath, wondering if he might amend his comment. "Hearts can only be willingly given, not conquered or contested." He stepped closer. "And for a heart willingly given, I am not opposed to such a thing . . ." He hovered near her, his body swaying closer and then back in small, almost imperceptible motions. Then he cleared his throat and looked away, seeming as surprised as she was to have uttered such a thing. "Someday."

The dancing began down the line, and Kate watched to understand what the lead would choose. Then she turned her attention back to Lord Dennison. "No slippers, no extravagant cravat . . . a simple black jacket? To what do I owe such mundane choices?"

"Mundane? Certainly not. Mundane sounds almost drab. And if you look, the jacket is new, the cravat crisp. I have taken extra care with my boots. And in all ways, I appear the proper gentleman. Mundane." He shook his head. "I prefer sensible."

She eyed him for a moment, but before she could respond, he continued.

"And honestly, I wish to talk of other things at this assembly. I have important ideas on my mind."

"Have you?"

"Yes. For example, when Parliament is next in session, what if I were to work toward actual change?"

Kate had to exhale twice before she knew what to say to him. "That sounds wonderful. What sorts of things would you want to change?"

"I don't know. So many things. For example, the tenants."

"Tenants?" She thought of how long she herself had been a tenant.

"They work, upkeep, and farm the land for generations. And yet live day to day at the mercy of the goodness of the landowner. Perhaps there is more we can do for the tenants."

She almost couldn't believe her ears, but this new Lord Dennison was a stunning replica of the first. He was superior in almost every regard.

"I'm sorry. Perhaps this type of conversation is as mundane as my choice in clothing?"

"Not at all. No. I am . . . most impressed and am at a loss as to how to congratulate you or encourage you. I wish more would exert themselves as you have." Kate had to take a breath. "Wow. I should like to assist."

"Assist?" Lord Dennison tipped his head to one side, in an almost mocking fashion.

"Certainly. Could I not?" She almost crossed her arms in deliberate defiance. "I have an interest in tenants, if you must know."

"Naturally. I didn't mean anything by my question. I would love assistance. I shall consider what to do about any of it. Perhaps the most important task will be in the House of Lords itself, won't it?" His open expression and hopeful tone made Kate smile, an expression full of hope of her own, that this lord was as good as she was hoping him to be.

When it was their turn to go through the motions of the dance, every touch between them seemed to linger, every opportunity to be close, face to face, was more amplified. Her heart called to him, or so she thought, with each sounding thump. And she could hardly school her features as she passed, when others would see, and any of those on the edge of the dance floor would think her ill or in love, neither of which she wanted assumed.

But when they were finished, she was not. And she dreaded the moment he would leave her at the side and she would dance with another.

But he did just that. He bowed over her hand, pressed his

lips on her knuckles, and thanked her, as if those moments together had not just altered her entire life.

She sighed. And then another lord, she knew not who, nor cared, bowed over her hand for another set.

The rest of the next two hours was full, every dance taken. Even though it was Kate's very wish going into the evening, now she cared little for anyone but Lord Dennison. Had his few comments of cares outside of fashion, of hoping to do good by tenants, meant so much to her as to ruin her for any other man?

It appeared they had.

And she didn't even mind.

She sought him out as her gaze flitted around the room. And every time she found him, he was looking in her direction. A couple times, he nodded his head, with a small, secretive smile, as if they shared something special together; other times, he just stared as long as she dared look, and the distance between them could have shrunk entirely as her world shifted and her whole being seemed to call out to his.

Of all the ridiculous notions.

Though it was ridiculously delicious.

She could dance no more with anyone other than Lord Dennison, so she escaped the dance floor into a room meant for cards. Many men played at the far end, but closer were tables set for whist and other parlor games, and then other tables where people sat conversing. Papers and flyers were strewn about, and Kate made a beeline for the first, hoping to see the latest *Her Lady's Whims and Fancies*.

Chapter Nine

Logan walked into the card room, looking for Miss Kate. But what he saw was something he didn't often see at an assembly room ball. Three tables of people doubled over in laughter. The other tables of cards had paused, and the whole room was paying attention to . . . something.

He stood still for a moment, trying to make out the cause. Then Lord Ballustrade looked his way, pointed, and shouted to the room, "And here's the man himself. Let's ask him who the paper is about."

All eyes turned to him. He lifted his chin and straightened his shoulders, the old, familiar arrogance settling in. Miss Kate's worried expression confused him. Out of the corner of his eyes, she looked . . . guilty even.

"What paper?" He stepped forward.

"This one here. *Her Lady's Whims and Fancies.*"

Logan snorted. "People accuse me of being in that column every week."

"True." Ballustrade lifted the paper. "But this gent here even looks like you."

"There's a drawing?"

"You've made the fashion plates." He held the paper up.

Of course, Logan couldn't see it from across the room, but something about this whole situation was really itching him in just the wrong way. What would the old Logan have done? Laughed? Celebrated? Read it aloud to everyone, certainly. As his gaze flitted through the room, he knew that's what they all expected of him. But . . . earlier today, after . . . Miss Kate, he just didn't want to play that part anymore. But this room, these people would eat him alive if he didn't act like it was his purpose all along. He felt his smile relax into the lazy, bored expression he usually wore. He gestured for a servant to bring him a drink, and loafed over to Ballustrade. "Let's see what we have here, shall we?"

When the paper opened up to his sight, it took every ounce of willpower to keep his expression bland. He smirked, ran his finger over an oaf of a man with an obscenely sized cravat blocking his head. Then he held the words closer. "Shall we read it?"

"Read, read, read, read." They were acting as though they were attending a fight at Jacksons, the women as well as the men. He didn't dare look at Miss Kate again, though her singular look of guilt had his interest piqued.

"Wedding, beautiful. Clothing and hairstyle unmatched by the ladies present." He bowed toward Miss Kate. "Et cetera, et cetera. Ah, here's the part where we hear about the gentlemen. And you're saying this is me?"

He skimmed the rest of the page. "My, oh my, this woman has been spurned."

The room filled with laughter.

"She says . . . some men can't help but aggrandize themselves. Through oversized cravats, overcolored slippers, overly loud insults, or over-pretentious attitudes. It might make many women wonder for what are they compensating." He felt his face heat. He couldn't even stop it, but he hoped to cover it. "There, you see. Spurned. Lashing out. I predict she is hiding away somewhere in a corner. See, a person cannot be so focused on finding fault unless she is truly unhappy with what she sees in the mirror." He laughed. And some did, too, but he suspected his comments hit too close to home for many of them. "At any rate, do you think I shall make every issue of *Her Lady's Whims and Fancies?*"

"I was mentioned as well," Ballustrade said.

"Were you?" Logan pretended to scan the paper anew, though he already had his finger on the spot. "Ah, here it is. The most glorious vest to be worn by any was certainly worn by a certain gentleman. True, indeed."

"And to think, today we've worn only our more regular clothing."

Logan downed the contents of his cup, not certain what he was drinking, and handed the paper back to Ballustrade. "You should frame that." He raised a hand. "Who has been so fortunate as to see this amazing of all vests?"

Surprisingly few hands went up in the air. So few, several trains of thought started running at once. Who had written this piece? How many people had seen the vest and witnessed his cravat and shoes? The person was, of course, in Brighton, or had been for the wedding. "This person missed an opportunity," Logan said.

"How so?" Ballustrade asked.

"Well, you yourself saw my jacket. The embroidery on that article of clothing is a piece of art."

"Too true. And if they don't include your face, the cravat effect is all but ruined."

"Whoever writes this *Whims and Fancies* is obviously a

spurned woman, as I said, but also an amateur—a fraud. She cannot know the first thing about fashion or presentation."

"I shall wear your cravat to prove it."

"You'd do that for me?"

"Certainly. And the others shall as well. We will be a Croatian cravat-wearing standoff against the spurned." Ballustrade held up his cup. "Who's with me?"

Most of the men in the room raised their cups.

"All who wish to wear the Croatian, send your valets to mine. He shall instruct you," Logan said.

Individual conversation seemed to pick up after that. Most in the room returned to their own pursuits, games continued, and people talked excitedly amongst themselves. But Logan struggled to feel normal. What was normal? He joined a table of men starting a new hand, so they dealt him in.

After a moment of jabbing about the cravat and the fashion plates, he examined his cards. "I'll be forming a new committee."

Most of the men continued studying their cards.

"I'd like us to examine our treatment of our tenants and shall bring it up in the House of Lords."

The man nearest snorted, and then the game began as though Logan was entirely inconsequential. Had they heard him at all?

"Shall we wear the Croatian cravat while presenting our ideas?" someone said.

Everyone at the table laughed.

They didn't think him capable of a serious act. Every one of the men assumed he was in jest. He finished the one hand, but then stood to leave before they could deal him in another. Pushing though those standing in the room, he left in a daze. He would walk home. Their townhome sat on The Strand as well.

He found his sister in the library with a book.

Soon, he was lost in another at her side. He could only thank his late father for the rescue. Here he felt useful, here his ideas had merit, here he learned from past great men how to be one himself. As he turned page after page, he tried to push the assembly ball out of his mind, but it hovered on the periphery no matter how many pages he turned.

He wore his most unremarkable clothing for weeks after, but everywhere he went, the men about him seemed to embrace his old ways. Every day, a new lord had mastered the Croatian cravat, and more and more, their jackets had turned brightly colored.

Another *Whims and Fancies* had come out the following week. This time highlighting Prinny as he exited the Royal Pavilion. Mention was made of Logan again. Not by name—never by name—but more interest was again sent in his direction. He walked along The Strand to get some air. Every time a man walked by with a Croatian cravat, he saluted Logan. Until he, the man who'd created that genius of a cravat, could no longer stand the sight of it. Over and over, the drawing of his cravat, filling the area that would be his face, flashed through his mind, and he began to find the whole thing ridiculous.

When he arrived home from his walk, he told his valet to ready his riding grear and then he went in search of Julia.

"I'm leaving for London," he told her.

"What? Already?"

"Yes, I have work to do, and none of it can be done here."

"Everyone you would want to talk to is here."

"But they don't wish to talk of anything other than my cravat, or my opinion of their jacket, or shoes, or fob."

Her eyes filled with sympathy. "If you leave, must I as well?"

"You've Aunt to keep you company while she sleeps. You could stay on as long as you like."

"And you won't be overly lonely if I do so?"

The loneliness ached like a continuous wound, but Logan shook his head. "I shall be far too distracted."

"Though much of your reading might be right here in this room."

He considered Julia's words. "You wish for me to stay."

She adjusted her skirts. "I was thinking we might have a dinner party and invite the Standish sisters before you go."

Miss Kate.

"I could delay my departure until then."

"Excellent. I'll get with cook."

As much as he wanted to ride out of Brighton that instant, just the mention of the Standish sisters reminded him that he hadn't explored his feelings for Miss Kate. She was the first woman to catch his eye since Olivia, the first to hold his attention. Indeed, their conversation the other evening was the best he'd had in ages, and she was in fact a part of the reason he had become so motivated to do good and be better.

But her expression at the assembly . . . Did she want nothing more to do with him? Was she tired of his antics? He'd been afraid to see her again, afraid of what he might see.

Though that was ridiculous. She was the most fashion-aware woman he'd ever seen. Her interest in Ballustrade's vest was almost comical to Logan.

But for some reason, she carried with her a higher purpose. Her focus seemed more intently driven, and he found himself desperately wanting to please her.

Was fashion not the way to do so? He guessed not, as odd as that seemed.

Once he'd donned his riding gear, he headed for the stables. A good, long run on Firestone would help clear his head.

Chapter Ten

Kate trailed her fingers along the trunks of old groves of trees that grew just down from the cliffs. She was heading her way to the brilliant blue skies and the lovely green grasses of the cliffs. She longed for the sea, and some quiet.

Lord Dennison's expression from the night at the assembly plagued her. Day in and out, she repeated that brief second when his reaction to the group was honestly and tenderly flitting from his face while he donned his mask. She kicked her toe into the dirt. Of all the wretched timing. He had just opened up to her, had just made plans to bring more meaning into his life. She'd seen a new life about him she'd never noticed before. And then her fashion plates.

She winced. Would she ever rid herself of this guilt?

When she walked out into the sunshine, she pulled her bonnet back up onto her head, hopefully hiding from the most direct rays. But she pushed onward and up the gentle slope that led out to the edge of the cliffs. She had an odd and exhilarating desire to hold her arms out at the edge and smile up into the wind and the sun. But concern wore her down. Her feet moved slowly.

She'd sent off her next batch of plates and her fashion tips and hints. These were more general, did not ring of gossip, and she actually enjoyed them much more, as she utilized some of her practiced habits to help women make the most of any dress, no matter how out of mode. She'd had years of practice making old castoffs look like the latest fashion.

Her heart cheered somewhat thinking of this new direction. If only she could do something to restore the damage she'd done to Lord Dennison.

She couldn't even face him.

When he'd left the room, he'd brushed past her as if he knew she were at fault. But how could he know?

And she'd been afraid to approach him ever since.

But she must.

As soon as the line of blue horizon reached her view, she smiled. On a glorious day like this, life had to get better.

The sound of hooves in the distance distracted her.

She squinted against the sun. A lone rider approached, but he was moving so quickly, she was sure he would gallop right past, which was just fine with her.

The blue changed colors the farther out into the deep water. The sky was its own shade. Kate held a hand up to further block the sun and studied the water. Small, white-capped waves rolled in one by one. White birds flew overhead, their sharp calls adding to the rushing sound from below. She crept forward, her very bones tingling from the height. But she wished to see the rocky shore below.

They hadn't explored the beaches lately, and she'd like to do so without a large picnic of onlookers. Perhaps there were treasures to collect—small animals or shells. The sounds lulled her into a calm that helped her focus on her next steps. Particularly, how to make amends to Lord Dennison.

"Miss Kate."

She spun around, her hand at her chest. "You . . . startled me."

Lord Dennison had dismounted from his horse, and approached with the reins in hand. He dipped his head in a small bow. "It is good to see you. Am I disturbing your solitude?" He moved closer, and she reached a hand over to rest on the horse's soft nose.

"You are most welcome to join me. I have been walking already for many hours."

"Have you? Do you often walk here?"

"Not here. Usually, I am down in the groves below the hill. Our castle estate property borders those trees. And I find great cool shade and solace as I walk among their ancient branches."

"So poetic."

"Perhaps I am of a notion to think of lovely words at the moment."

"Are you?" Lord Dennison considered her. "Shall we walk? Or sit?"

He pointed to a large rock outcropping that sat back enough from the cliff edge so as to feel safe.

"I'd love to sit for a moment. And then, I was considering just how I might walk down to the water's edge."

"Were you?" He followed behind.

Once Kate was seated, he joined her, almost touching. They both stared out at the water for a moment, and then he chuckled. "I've been avoiding society."

She didn't need to ask why. And her guilt churned inside. "I as well."

"Have you? Why?"

"Something doesn't sit well with me right now, and I'm

trying to figure it out. I'm assuming you are hiding because of *Her Lady's Whims and Fancies?*"

"Partly. The fashion article painted me in a most exaggerated fashion, but, I fear, accurately."

She shook her head.

"True. How can you ever portray the full measure of a man?" Lord Dennison said. "The author merely chose to exaggerate a quirk of mine. It does not represent me."

"But will the others let you grow past it?"

He shook his head. "Not here, I don't think. Not when they are all in a loyal manner supporting my cravat." He laughed. "Have you seen?"

"No, I haven't."

"They are teaching their valets to tie the Croatian cravat and wearing it everywhere, coming to find me to show their support. They will continue in London, they say."

"That's sweet, in a way."

"I suppose."

"And your efforts for tenants?"

"You've hit upon the very problem. I cannot speak of anything beyond the lighthearted without people turning away or assuming I'm in jest."

"Tell me of Olivia."

Her question jarred him. She could tell. His face contorted for a moment, and then the mask of boredom slid across his face.

She braced herself for some response that would send him further in hiding. But instead, he stared out at the sea so long, she suspected he might not answer.

"I thought I had found the love of my life. She had seemed so accepting of me, of all my advances, my small gifts . . . the talks we would have. She bore her soul, or so I thought. I assumed I was the only one courting her. I assumed she cared." Lord Dennison's pained face made Kate almost wish she hadn't asked. To spare him the pain of retelling.

"But when I bent on one knee, she said no." He turned to her, the pain in his eyes sharp. "I never imagined she would say no. She gave me every reason to believe her love as powerfully consuming as mine."

"What happened to her?"

"She married someone she'd known since they were young. I could have never known she had such an acquaintance. He returned from touring the continent, proposed immediately, and she accepted."

Kate tried to imagine his pain but could not. "What a wretched thing to do to another."

"You've perhaps not come across some of the truly careless among us, but such is to be expected, I'm afraid. The Whims and Fancies of the world will never consider the heart of another as dear as they should."

Her involuntary wince shook her body.

"Are you unwell?"

"I . . . I am well. Though I think I would like to walk." She stood, fighting every inclination to run.

Lord Dennison stood as well and continued speaking, "And so I have learned. We all have our secrets. When is there an opportunity to tell our deepest desire or thoughts to another? So I'm unsure I will ever be able to ask again."

She stepped closer to walk at his side. "Ask?"

"Propose." The flit of desperate sadness that crossed his eyes for a moment clenched in her own heart. "I'd like to. But I don't know if I can."

"I think I understand." They walked farther along for a moment, Lord Dennison leading his horse beside him, with only the waves to entertain them.

"How can we know another?" Kate said. She had never considered such a thing.

"Some don't care to know the people they will marry. They don't plan on love matches. The marriage is more of convenience than anything else."

"Might you consider that some day?"

"I might." He studied the side of her face, but she could not look at him yet. She didn't trust her expression. "And you? Might you consider such a thing?"

"I had hoped . . ." She studied the ground at her feet. "I had hoped for love, or at least warm affection. I had hoped such feelings would grow over time, even in marriage. I had hoped so many things." She shook her head. "And then I have told myself for years to dash those hopes, to consider any offer from any man as the best I would ever get. Only recently do I recognize I may have some choice or freedom in the matter." She stopped walking. "There was a time when I desperately worked and studied and planned for a way to support myself and my sisters." She pleaded silently for him to someday in some way understand why she did what she did for the newspaper. Perhaps one day, when he discovered it was she who had so carelessly dealt with the heart of another—his heart—when he discovered it was she, greater understanding might warm him toward a matter of forgiveness?

"But now?" Lord Dennison asked.

"Now, I suppose I am free to marry for love." She sighed, the sound lost in the wind. "But is such a thing truly possible? As you said, how would we ever come to know another well enough?"

"Love is easy. Finding another who loves you in return, that has been the elusive bit for me."

They approached the edge, where a path led down to the beach. "Might we walk along the water?" Kate suggested.

Lord Dennison peered over the edge and then out to sea. "It might be more enjoyable if we were to ride."

Her smile revealed her, and he laughed. "Ride, we shall." He stepped closer. "Might I assist you?" He indicated with his hands that he wished to place them at her waist.

"Yes."

As soon as his palms were at her side, he paused, standing close, and looked down into her face. His grip softened, his fingers nothing more than a caress of the sweetest kind. But then his soft words, "Are you ready?" returned her immediately to the task at hand.

"Yes, I think so."

He lifted her as though she weighed nothing and then slipped up on the horse behind her. She rode sidesaddle, and the fit was very tight behind her, but his arms came forward as he held the reins to her front, and she smiled.

His words in her ear were breathy, enticing, his deep voice rumbling through her. "Is this acceptable?"

She nodded.

"Is it . . . nice?"

Her cheeks flamed. She wondered if her neck felt as hot. But she nodded again.

His lips, so close to her ear, so near her skin, whispered again, "Then I shall continue." He adjusted the reins.

She leaned back more of her weight against him, and he guided the horse down the path.

Chapter Eleven

Kate in his arms. Kate putting her trust in him. *Miss Kate*, Logan corrected, but went right back to calling her Kate in his mind. Her soft arms, the lovely smell of violets that filled the air around them, the gooseflesh on her skin that he doubted she knew he could see all combined to do things to him he hadn't felt in a long time.

Not even with Olivia had he been so captivated. Loved her, he had, but that love had felt so juvenile compared to this new rush of interest, respect, and plenty of desire he felt for the intriguing woman in his arms.

The horse stepped carefully, surefooted, though the path was steep in places.

Kate gripped his arms at times and shifted her weight farther back into him.

When they finally reached the bottom of the path, he was well on his way to complete fascination with a woman he knew little about. He'd done the same with Olivia, and he could not do any more damage to his heart. Was Kate as intrigued in him as he her? He had no way of knowing. Was she a decent sort of person? She seemed so, but again, he had no way of knowing. Olivia had seemed all those things, and with the death of that relationship had died his confidence in his ability to read a person.

He dismounted off the horse and handed Kate down, and then led his stallion to wander in the grasses. "The rocks aren't good for his hooves."

She nodded. "He's a beautiful animal."

The horse's black coat shone in the sunlight.

"He is. We've been through a lot together."

Logan held his arm for Kate to take, and when she leaned on him as they made their way down the rocky shore, he found himself standing taller, feeling more protective, wanting to be important to her. "Shall we talk about our dreams?"

"Our dreams?" She frowned, a tiny, delicate arc to her brows, her lips pushed forward in the smallest pout. "You first."

"Dreams change, don't they? How about we start with those from our youth?"

This seemed the most agreeable choice to Kate. Was she reluctant to share about herself? "How about we take turns asking questions?" Logan continued. "To be fair, each question has to have a complete answer."

Her face went white for a moment, but then she nodded, a slight, brazen glint in her eye. "I am willing. How about I ask the first question?"

"Excellent." He held up a finger. "But this new, daring face you are making . . . remember that I will retaliate with an equally bold question if that is the direction you choose."

"I understand."

Her calculating smile made him laugh. What was she going to be to him? He didn't know. But he was sure enjoying finding out. They moved along closer to the water. "While you are thinking, today really is a delectable day. Perfect in all regards," Logan said.

"I quite agree. Now stop. I know my question. Tell me the most daring thing you did as a child."

"Oh, that is simple but you might consider me a danger to myself and my family."

"This does sound interesting."

"Thank heavens you are not the editor for *Whims and Fancies*. I'd have a devil of a time if this story got out to all and sundry."

Kate stumbled on the rocks.

"Careful. If you wish, we can move more slowly."

"Yes, thank you." She took a moment more, perhaps to compose herself. And then she looked up at him, one hand on top of her bonnet, which was blowing in the wind. "Are you going to share?"

"Yes, of course." He stood taller. "My tutor." He grimaced. "I loathed the man, but he pushed me to greatness every day." He eyed her, not attempting to show any remorse. "Should I be grateful to him now that I'm older and wiser, as they say?"

"The answer to that depends entirely on what you are about to tell me, I'd imagine."

"Too true. So the day came and went that I was to have the entirety of one particular Shakespearean sonnet memorized."

"Dreadful."

"Yes. My nine-year-old self had decided once and for all to have none of it. Julia had no such assignment. She was coddled and pampered, her main tasks learning the fashions of the day and how best to present herself."

"Sounds like the beginning of your cravat fascination."

Logan stopped and stared, knowing his mouth was dropping open but ignoring the inclination to shut it. "I've never once given the reasons any thought, but I do believe you are correct.

Spending all of one's childhood wishing your life to be as easy as your twin's could do that to a fellow."

"Yes, perhaps. I interrupted. Do continue."

"You seem so interested in the failings of a lad. Have you something to gain from my exploits?"

"What? No. How could I?" Kate's laugh sounded forced, nervous, and he studied her for a moment. She shook her head. "I have nothing to gain. Would you like me to answer a question first?"

"No, I wish to answer. If someone on this beach would allow?"

"Certainly. I allow. We are all allowing." She waved her hand around at the empty space around them.

"As I was saying . . ." He winked. "I grew tired of my assignments, the rote memorization, the grueling math, all of it."

"As most young lads do."

"Precisely." Logan meant to simply pat Kate's hand, which rested on his arm, but as his fingers came to rest over hers, he let his hand remain. The gentle pressure, the simple feeling of companionship stayed his hand, and if he had anything to say about it, would have kept him there forever. He cleared his throat. "I decided I would show my tutor who was really in control of our lessons." He stared out at the sea, deliberately pausing.

"And?"

Then he grinned. "You are fun to tell a story to, I must admit. And I wrote a sonnet myself. Dedicated to his odious lessons, to the odious nature of the man himself, the odious idea that I would have to study at all when most boys my age were playing by the creek, and anything odious in general."

She laughed. "That would have been way more work than simply memorizing Shakespeare."

"But much more fun. And would you like to know what I titled it?"

"Let me guess . . . *Ode to the Odious?*"

"Oh, that is clever. Not quite. I called it simply *Odious.*"

"You did not."

"I did. And I still have it memorized. If someday, I feel we are close enough friends, I shall recite it to you."

"Oh, that would be too good. Yes. I shall await the day we have grown intimate enough."

Logan studied Kate, waiting for her to correct herself, but she seemed perfectly comfortable with the idea that they would grow closer . . . and in intimate ways.

They walked along, close enough to the water to jump away now and again as a stray waved rolled higher up on the shore than the others. "And now my question for you," Logan said.

The eyes she turned up to him suddenly begged to be closer to him. Suddenly, his whole body wished it so, and he had to physically force himself to stay put on the sand, walking calmly at her side. How could one woman have such a hold on a man? Olivia did not have this same power.

Now that he was beginning to know what it felt like to know Kate, he was beginning to question what he felt for Olivia. But there was no denying the hurt and pain of Olivia's refusal.

He considered Kate. "What is the most shameful thing you have ever done?"

She teetered, and Logan steadied her on the rocks. "Though rocks are not as dirty as sand, they are certainly much more cumbersome," he said.

"They certainly are." She studied him for a moment, then smiled. "I shall speak of my youth as you have."

"Excellent."

"I call this *The Tale of the Missing Slippers.*"

"Oh, will it be a sonnet?"

"Not quite."

"Excellent. Continue."

"June, the eldest of my sisters, always had the nicest things." Kate looked up into his face, and suddenly, years of pain and worry were obvious marks he was surprised not to have noticed before now. "When we still had our parents and many nice things, she was gifted a new pair of slippers."

"Naturally, this story will have something to do with slippers."

"Oh, too true. As you know our joint affinity for fine shoes."

"Too true."

"I envied those slippers. I wanted them so badly, my toes hurt."

"Your . . . toes?"

"Yes, from longing."

Logan half-nodded, delighted in the tale.

"And so one day, while she was out on a walk . . ."

"Not wearing her new slippers."

"Precisely. I borrowed them."

"Of course. So far, I'm almost disappointed that this is the most shameful thing you have done."

Guilt crossed Kate's face, and Logan was reminded of the moment in the cardroom where she had looked the same. Her empathy knew no bounds. He squeezed the hand that rested beneath his.

"There is more."

"Ho, ho!"

"I wore them around the house to complete my lessons." She sighed. "They were more beautiful than anything I owned, I was certain of it. When the governess was looking elsewhere, I would poke the toe out from underneath my dress so that I might admire them."

"Naturally."

"But soon, lessons were over, and I was dismissed, and I forgot I was wearing them. I took to the outdoors."

"Oh, dear. I suddenly know where this is going."

"And ruined them."

Logan nodded, sadly. "Death to all good slippers in just such a way."

"And then I returned them to her closet without a word."

"You didn't."

"I did."

He waited. When she said nothing, he asked, "And what came of it?"

"Nothing."

"Nothing at all?"

"No. June never complained. Of course, she never wore them again, but I don't think anyone knew."

"Did June suspect?"

"I'm certain, but she said nothing, and true to her nature, sacrificed any thought she might have had of revenge, justice, or even a replacement pair of slippers."

"I would have grown up a heathen with such a woman as my sister."

Kate laughed. "You can be sure many times I've felt so."

Her nose wiggled when she laughed. Realizing such a thing was wreaking pleasant war on Logan's insides. What else could he say to see such an exquisite expression on her face?

They approached a thick log. "Shall we sit?" Logan asked. He slipped off his jacket and laid it down on the wood for her.

"What? No. Your jacket."

He shook his head. "I care not for such things."

When she stared with open-mouthed disbelief, he shook his head. "I don't. It is more a façade than anything." Why was he admitting such a thing?

"If you're certain . . ." She stepped closer. Had she? Or had he? They were so close, he could count the freckles on her creamy skin. Three. And so perfectly placed.

He reached out to aid with a stray hair in the wind. "I'm certain."

"Me, too."

The certainty of something seemed to flow between them. A solid, sure path. But Logan couldn't resist the tease. "You're certain, are you?"

Kate blinked, and then swatted him. "Oh, stop. See, I shall sit upon your jacket, ruining it." She approached. Then shook her head. "I cannot."

He laughed. "I have no cares for this jacket," he amended. "I care more for your comfort than I do the bit of clothing. Please. Sit. Ruin."

Gingerly, she placed a bit of her weight on it. "It does feel nice to rest my feet."

"I've been a dunce of the highest form. I forgot. You'd been walking for hours before I happened upon you."

She waved as though it were nothing. "I could walk hours more, but the rocks make a difference, don't they?"

"They do." How singular to walk with a woman who complained not once, about anything, who enjoyed his conversation, who laughed easily, and who, in all her memory, carried the misuse of slippers as her most shameful moment. He studied her.

"What?" Kate asked.

"What, what?"

"You're staring. Your smile. I'm beginning to wonder what is racing about in your thoughts."

"If you must know, I was merely considering on the singular pleasure of having you all to myself on this deserted beach."

Her cheeks colored prettily.

"And now, I am further pleased to have created this lovely effect. But never fear. Though I will sit beside you, I have no designs on your propriety."

"Not even a small design?" Her eyebrow raised in a daring challenge, and Logan couldn't make her out.

"Are you . . ." He studied her. "No. You're not. You're teasing."

She tipped her head and laughed. "I'm teasing . . ." But her expression and her voice trailed off, and he wondered.

Chapter Twelve

✿

What was Kate thinking? Was she inviting scandal? Absolutely not. Heaven help them. She prayed that he would not take her comments as invitation to do anything untoward. She shook her head. He wouldn't. Somehow, she knew Lord Dennison to be the perfect gentleman.

Too perfect.

What was wrong with her? Thank the stars that one's thoughts were not paraded about in the air. Especially during this conversation. How many times had guilt nearly overtaken her?

Too many.

He must never know. At one time, she thought to come clean, apologize, but now, after this stretch of sand in their past, she couldn't let him ever know. The admiration that had so quickly overtaken his expression would be replaced by disappointment, hurt, betrayal.

No.

He must never know.

Keeping things secret should be simple enough. Her own sisters didn't know. Though she suspected Amelia knew. She wouldn't let on. And as soon as she could, Kate would quit her work for *Whims and Fancies*.

Could she? No.

What if she were ever in a situation again with no money or food or place to live except provided by others?

While this turmoil ran through her mind, she tried to place the calmest and most congenial expression on her face.

Lord Dennison sat beside her and lifted her hand with his. "May I?"

She nodded.

"I find I am quite charmed by this whole conversation. Should we ask another question?" he said.

"Certainly. It's my turn." She pushed unpleasant thoughts from her mind. "Now, I would like to know what you hope to be, when you're settled and . . . established in your life?"

"Married?"

"Yes, or, I don't know, older."

"Ah, the question of where do I see myself when we're all grown?" He laughed. "Though it is a bit rough on a chap to realize that even though he does very little of substance with his life, he is well and truly already grown."

"Not at all. How many of our associates are the same? I'm interested to hear where you see yourself . . . eventually."

"Fair question." He tapped his fingers on her palm, and she enjoyed every sensation that raced up her arm. "We have an estate in the north of England. It abuts the ocean." He waved his hand out to the grand blue to their front. "The water is not as calm. The beach is full of large rocks. But the view is the most beautiful in the world. The house has gardens and trees and a beautiful situation. But everything else around is rugged and full of energy. I love it up there. I would like to be settled in our rooms, my wife and I, with our children in theirs, looking out over the wide expanse of ocean every morning with our breakfast trays."

Kate couldn't swallow. No bit of moisture remained in her mouth. What a beautiful dream. Breakfast. Simple. Perfect. *That's my dream.* Had it been her dream before she arrived on the beach that morning? Not that she knew of. But now that it had been spoken aloud, she could only yearn for such a moment every day of her life until it came to be. After a moment, Lord Dennison turned to her. "Perhaps that is too simple, too boring a life for some." His voice trailed off.

She forced herself to gain some semblance of use of her voice. "Not at all. I am speechless with wonder at such a plan. I didn't know. I hadn't thought such a thing could be so beautiful." She couldn't even hide the yearning in her voice. "I would love that dream to be mine." Before she could suck back in her words, she froze.

But he put his hand behind her on the old trunk and leaned closer. "Would you?"

She nodded, once again without a single word. Her mouth was so incredibly dry. She licked her lips. His eyes dropped to her mouth immediately. She swallowed again, feeling the motion large and forced, but his mouth, his lips, were soft and thick, his jaw strong, and he was suddenly so very close.

His lashes waved across his eyes, which crinkled in the corners, his smile spreading happiness through her. He lifted another strand of wayward hair and ran his fingers along the side of her face. "Perhaps." The words sent rumbles of pleasure through her. Perhaps. Then he lifted his chin and placed one soft kiss on her forehead.

She leaned into his kiss. "Oh."

He cupped her cheek with his hand, tipped his head, and pressed his lips to hers. Just once, softly. And the thrill of unspoken promises rushed through her in happy waves. She opened her eyes. His shining happiness grinned back. "Tell me all the things that make you happy," he said.

"Pardon?" Kate's mind, in a daze, could not register mere words as anything important to grab ahold of, but after blinking twice, she nodded. "You." Then she laughed and sat up straighter, missing immediately their intimate closeness. She shook her head, as if such a thing would ever help her think clearly again. "And . . . my sisters, when we are all together. A beautiful hairstyle. Art. I love when the colors balance in a painting. A simple walk on the beach. Wind in my hair when it is free of all pins." She laughed.

"I wouldn't mind such a thing if you care to release this thick, dark beauty from its prison."

She laughed, eyeing him with a question. Did she dare? She would return looking like an absolute hoyden. But what did that matter? Who would be there to see? She lifted her bonnet and handed it to Lord Dennison.

The intimacy of such a gesture was not lost on her, or him, if the darkening of his eyes was any indication. Then she began by tugging pins. But some were stuck. And she had no mirror to see, and she was halfway into wreaking havoc on her hair. No going back now. "Oh, dear."

"Might I assist?" His voice was husky, deep, close.

"I would very much appreciate it."

As soon as his fingers were trailing through her hair, seeking out pins and handing them to her, Kate was full of happy tingles of expectation. Every brush against her head, every movement of hair by his hands filled her with one thing. Desire. She wanted Lord Dennison in her life. She wanted him near. And she wanted him to always run his fingers through her hair. Each pin was an unhappy countdown to the moment when he would stop. He trailed his fingers over her head, seeking any stray pins, and then moved the lot of it off her shoulders to trail back behind her.

"Your hair is magnificent. In case I never see such glory on you again, I am happy for this moment."

She shook her head, the wind catching her hair and sending further waves of pleasure through her. "This is lovely. I think all women should wear their hair thus." She ran fingers through, untangling some remaining knots, and then stood. "Let's dance!" She ran out across the beach with her arms out to her side and spun in great circles.

Lord Dennison, laughing, joined her, and they weaved together, laughing and dancing their own music-less tribute to the freedom of the air and the water and the bright blue sky.

After a moment, breathless, Kate stopped. "And now, I must replace my bonnet."

He looked up at the sun. "Ah yes, freckles."

"Freckles."

"Perhaps *Whims and Fancies* shall declare freckles to be on mode?" He laughed.

But his words shook her.

"Not likely, I'm afraid." Though she tried to keep her earlier feelings of careless freedom close, she knew it was hopeless. Her shoulders drooped as she followed Lord Dennison back to their things.

His arms were strong. Without his jacket, she could see more the definition in his arms, and the power he carried as he walked—the strength in his chest and arms sent happy shivers through her. Really, he was everything a man should be. All those months of admiring him from afar had been merited. And she now could only wish she deserved such a man.

She would make things right. She must. "How—how are things after that time in the card room?" Kate's voice shook. She dreaded his response.

Just as she feared, his shoulders stiffened. But then they relaxed, and he turned with a ready smile. "I don't even care."

"You don't?"

Lord Dennison shook his head. "I have work to do to convince the others that I have a brain working on complexities in between these shoulders whose use is far greater than simply to hold the jacket, true to form, on my body." He lifted his jacket off the trunk, not even bothering to shake it or brush it off. "But I will work to do so. The true test will be when I talk to my friends from Oxford and the other active members of the House of Lords." He looked about to say more, but he stopped. "Forgive me. I'm speaking without thinking. Most of this is probably nothing you're interested in."

"Oh, but I am. Remember, it is I who hope to aid in the tenant considerations as well."

"Too true. Too true." He reached for her hand. "And now, loathe as I am to leave this idyllic paradise, I feel there are some who would begin to ask after you by now."

Kate sighed, knowing his words to be true. "I don't think they are as yet alarmed, but I'm sure the question of where I am has been asked about by now."

"And I shall return you in this gloriously disheveled state?" His eyebrow rose, and then he tugged her closer, wrapping his arms around her back. "Thank you. I've never enjoyed myself more." His lips, warm and comforting on her forehead, sent a trickle of peace through her raging dissatisfaction. Then he tugged her again, and they made their way along the beach.

Once back up on his horse, she used her pins and her hands to wrap her hair in a simple bun at the base of her neck.

Lord Dennison's wistful expression made her laugh.

"Please understand. Your hair off your neck leaves it in glorious view. That creamy skin. Do you know it was the first thing I noticed about you?"

"My creamy skin?" Remembering his comments, she laughed. "Or was it my wasteful attention to fashion at the absence of all else?"

"Oh please, do not repeat my words. I say this now so you will understand the true thoughts of my heart. I was enchanted by all that wasteful attention. Your several curls placed in a beguiling tease, bouncing along at the base of such a long and creamy stretch of skin, begged to be caressed, if not kissed. And that's the truth of it."

She sucked in a breath as he climbed up on the horse behind her, enveloping her in an embrace.

His horse carried them back up to the top of the hill, on the cliffs, and then down on the other side toward the road.

"Will you be riding with me all the way to the castle?" Kate asked.

His chin on her shoulder made her smile. "I could."

"When will I see you again?" She knew she sounded so brazen, so forward, but he had kissed her, after all. Hopefully, it meant as much to him?

"Who says I'm leaving your side?" His warm chuckle did wonderful, tight things to her insides.

"Shall I tell the staff to make a room for you, then?" Kate joked, but only partly.

"Might I call on you every day during the time any of the other lords might arrive to think they can have a bit of your smiles?"

"Certainly." She smiled.

"And perhaps during the dinner hour, to share of your good cook's meals?"

"That can be arranged."

"And then perhaps, we might have a picnic with you and all the sisters and the Granburys in two days' time?"

"We would love such a thing. I'll tell the boys they are welcome also?"

"Yes, of course. Perhaps we can make use of this delightful grove?" They entered the cool shade of the ancient trees.

"What a splendid idea. Yes. I shall let them know." She turned to him. "What are we doing here?"

Lord Dennison looked as though he might laugh off the sincerity of her question, but then he paused. "Does this count as your turn?"

Her mouth tugged into a smile. "Yes."

"Then I will answer. I want to know you. I want us to keep having conversations like the one today, and I don't mind how long they take or how many months we spend, because I wish to know everything about you. And when we are comfortable, perhaps . . ." He pressed his lips to her neck. "Perhaps we talk further."

Kate nodded, slowly.

"My question is what perhaps every man in love would like to know."

"Oh yes? And what is that?"

"Is this really happening for you like it is for me?" His voice caught, and he looked away. But not before she saw an incredible fear and vulnerability cross over his face.

The dear. Her heart wrenched in two on his behalf. She vowed to never, ever hurt him, to never allow what had happened with Olivia to happen to him again. She twisted farther in the saddle toward him, reached a hand out behind his neck, and pulled him to her. When her lips met his, she tried to communicate her promise that his heart was safe with her. She captured his mouth, pulling at his lips, answering any fear he had with her surety that she would never leave him.

At first, he seemed stunned, hesitant, but after only a moment, his arm circled her and shifted her at a more comfortable angle, and he responded. Love poured through her. Her arms tightened around him, and for a long moment, she forgot where she was.

The horse shifted, and the sounds of birds around them, the rushing of the waves in the distance, a twig cracking all reached her ears. She released her grip on his neck, amazed at her brazen and almost wanton behavior. She daren't look in Lord Dennison's face just yet. As she studied her hands, his low murmur sent comfort through her. "Now, that's a kiss."

She could hear his smile before she turned again to see it. What she saw made her laugh outright. "Now, I've never seen a man as happy as you look."

He stretched his hands high above his head. "And why should I not be?"

Kate knew her face shone crimson, but she didn't even care. "I have no idea." She faced the front again. "Take me home, Lord Dennison. But not too close. I think I'll walk up to the house."

"Embarrassed of me?"

"In a way." She laughed again. "Let's just . . . Let's go."

His arms pulled her back up tight against him as he jiggled the reins. "Yes, ma'am."

She smiled, leaning up against him, wishing for this moment to last forever.

When he lifted her off the horse and climbed down to stand in front of her, he reached for her hand and placed his lips upon the back of her glove. The action felt so tame, so lacking compared to the attention of his lips from earlier. He winked, as if he knew exactly what she was thinking, and then hopped back up on his horse. "I'll watch from here."

"Thank you." She stared for a moment, drinking in their time together, hoping to bottle it up inside to remember later, and then turned to leave.

Chapter Thirteen

L ogan watched Kate walk the rest of the way through their back pasture into the gardens that surrounded the castle. From there, he knew she would walk by their lovely fountain and on into the house.

He couldn't quite think properly. At least, that's what he thought as he attempted to make sense of the swirl of emotions shuddering through him. Had he fallen in love with Miss Kate Standish? In one afternoon?

Certainly, not. But his feelings were more powerful than anything he'd ever felt for Olivia, or any woman. Kissing Kate was . . . He had no words. He was changed. But one thing he knew, and that was he would spend every waking moment trying to know this woman, to win her over completely, and then ask her . . . He couldn't think the words, couldn't admit what he was thinking. The thought of another rejection, or her refusal, was too much. So he stopped there. It was too early for such thoughts anyway.

Then he grinned to himself. At least he knew he loved

kissing the woman, an important part of any marriage, in his mind. He shook his head in happiness. "What a woman." The words spoken aloud sounded funny to his ears, but not his heart. He'd never experienced such an afternoon with a woman. And when she'd taken control of their kiss, when she'd wiped every fear from his mind, he'd been nearly overwhelmed. "Wow." He clucked his tongue, and his horse turned back. Julia would be wondering about their plans in the library. He'd told her they had a standing appointment.

And she'd be pleased about a picnic with the Standishes as well. Did his sister have interests here in Brighton? She didn't seem as though she did. He knew countless lords would be pleased to make her an offer, for her dowry alone, but he hoped for something more. Perhaps his sister could have her heart turned and fall in love.

Walking his horse back, he went over his conversation with Kate. He looked forward to many more. And he did have a bit of a puzzle to figure out. He couldn't put his finger on it. But Kate did not seem happy . . . She was, but then, she wasn't. And now that his interests seemed to be so tied to hers, he could not sit easy until he discovered the cause.

Logan hurried home, stabled his horse, and made his way to the library. As soon as his sister saw him, she stood up. "What is this?"

"What is what?"

"This supremely happy look on your face?" She approached him and made a show of circling him once. "What has happened?"

He laughed. "Don't be ridiculous. Though I am feeling supremely happy, if you must know."

She waved him back over to their chairs. "Do tell."

He considered her a moment. Did he wish to share anything

so soon? Would the fates jinx his efforts? No. "I happened upon Kate at the beach."

"Oh? And Kate, is it now?"

"Quite." His smile grew, and he could do nothing about it.

"This is too good." Julia settled back into her chair. "Tell me everything."

"I think she returns my feelings with equal strength."

"Excellent. And?"

And? There was no "and." That was all that mattered to Logan. Well, almost all. "When she talks of important things, her lip puckers right here." He indicated the spot with his finger. "It's fascinating to watch such a thing. She fits perfectly in my arms, and we talked of only nothing for hours on end. I could never tire of her company."

Julia squealed and clapped her hands together once. "This is wonderful news." She moved to the desk and pulled out a sheaf of paper.

"What are you doing?"

"I shall invite her for tea."

"Oh, excellent. I think she'd be very interested to see the history of her castle that we found."

"Good idea. And you do remember we are to dine there as well?"

"Certainly, but one cannot see too much of the woman whose lip puckers while she talks of important things." Julia snorted and kept writing.

"Oh, do stop, or I won't tell you a thing."

"Right. We're being serious."

Nothing would ever get Logan to share some of their moments: the feel of her hair in his hands, or the embrace on his horse, or the feel of her mouth on his. Those thoughts were for him alone.

He spent the rest of the late afternoon hours and evening reading or playing cards with Julia. When they were heading to bed for an early night, she leaned into his side. "Thank you for today," she said.

"Yes, you, too. We should spend evenings like this one more often."

"I agree. I don't know how strong your feelings are for Miss Kate, but I'm half in love with her already if she can bring this much contentment to your life."

Logan squeezed Julia back and thought about her words during the whole of his valet's ministrations. Long after his servant had left, he stood at the window, staring out on the ever busy Strand. If he stood in the corner of his window and looked to the side, he knew the ocean to be in the dark space beyond the buildings and store fronts.

Kate's acceptance of their invitation to come to tea tomorrow had already been received. He turned to his bed, his eyes closing with the happy anticipation of Kate here in their home.

Logan spent the morning hours writing letters to his friends from Oxford. They had not yet responded to his initial conversation, but he had discovered more information to share with them and hoped that their responses were already on their way at any rate. Perhaps he could convince them to come to Brighton. He knew most of them to be in London. How much more simple for him to travel to town . . . but he couldn't bring himself to leave—not yet.

The hour approached for them to receive Kate. Julia had decided to set up all of their tea and extras from cook in the library.

"Excellent choice," Logan said.

"I quite agree, and since there is much we want to show her here, I figured why not?"

She had taken extra care with the presentation. A small vase of their roses, freshly cut, sat in the center of the extra desk they were using to set the tray and its contents.

When the butler announced Kate, Logan could hardly stay his pace as he hurried to her side. "Welcome." He bowed over her hand, enjoying the soft color to her cheeks, the warmth in her returning smile, her very presence in his home.

"Thank you." She curtseyed. "I was so pleased to receive the invitation. Julia, thank you. This looks lovely."

"I admit to having a little more fun with the presentation than I would usually," Julia said.

"And here in the library." Kate turned to see it. "What an amazing collection. I would spend many an afternoon right here."

Julia took Kate's hands in her own and led her into the room. "Which is just precisely what we have been doing. You would be a welcome inclusion to our party."

"Thank you."

Kate's eyes lingered long enough on the books that Logan laughed. "Shall we start with the books, then?" he asked.

Julia laughed as well. "It looks that way. I admit that Logan and I have very different likes and dislikes when it comes to our selections. But we do know of some that would be of particular interest to you."

Kate's eyes widened, and Logan loved that she would be intrigued. By his books, no less.

As they walked down each aisle, her fingers trailed on the shelves, sometimes caressing the bindings. "This is incredible. June would love this room as well."

"When she returns, we will include her in an invitation. Please feel at ease in reading any you like," Logan said.

Kate nodded.

They led her down the aisle that contained the early history of Brighton. "We have found some interesting details about your castle," he told her.

"Oh?" She grinned. "I'm most intrigued by the history of my castle. Did I mention the box of clothes I found? And we have found other things. The place is so immense, new mysteries are showing up all the time."

He lifted the most intriguing tome. "Come, let's have a look at this."

"Yes, and tea as well." Julia gestured back to their spread.

"Certainly." Logan led Kate back to a simple seating they had arranged. Julia poured the tea.

Kate. Here in his favorite room in the home, with Julia at his side. He watched her every sip, every enjoyment of the crumpets or the sandwiches, reveled in every compliment she gave to Julia.

Then he laughed at himself.

"And what is so funny?" Julia asked.

"Oh, this is not the laugh of anything humorous. This laugh is enjoyment, pure and simple."

Kate's eyes lifted to his, and for a moment, their communion across the table was powerful. It coursed between them as a current from the ocean and seemed to rise in a rush to heaven.

Logan lifted the historical tome. "So it says here that the Normans built your castle."

"That's what we suspected. William the Conqueror himself."

He flipped through the pages. "Yes. He was hoping his wife would come here to live. He built it with all the latest comforts of the time."

Kate laughed. "Such as they were."

"Precisely. And then he lived there, briefly, but his wife came for only one year and then returned to be the regent in their dukedom in France." He turned the page. "But in that one year, they gave birth."

Kate leaned closer.

"And the record is unclear to whom." He flipped to the back of the book. "See here, this chart. It shows the lineage of William the Conqueror, but there is some lack of clarity as to the ages of the sons, and there is a question about an additional daughter. See here." He pointed to a blank space in the list of children. "The footnote says that there is a good amount of evidence that this final child was a girl." He flipped back to the pages about the castle. "However, there is nothing to indicate whether or not it's true."

"This is all very exciting! What if there is a lost daughter of William the Conqueror? Someone history has forgotten, born in our castle." Kate's eyes turned dreamy. "I would love to read this."

"Certainly." Logan handed it over.

Julia lifted her cup. "So, are you descended from William himself?"

Kate studied her own cup for a moment. "We think so. We aren't entirely certain in what manner we are related to him. We do have a loose connection through Henry I, William the Conqueror's son. He had a daughter, Matilda. And we have been told that she is our grandmother many times over." She laughed. "But some of the connection is very vague during those times."

"And something about this is very important to you." Logan said it as the fact it was. He knew just by watching her that something simmered just below the surface.

She puffed out a breath. "It is. This may sound . . . odd. But for many years, we as a family have felt like we don't really fit."

She paused, and he and Julia shared a glance, but he sat as quietly as he could, hoping Kate would continue.

"Our parents died, and we were immediately shuffled out of our childhood home by the inheritor of the estate. Sent to live with a distant cousin, someone we called Uncle."

"Was it too terrible?" Julia reached for her hand.

"I was young, and no. We loved Uncle. He became our parental figure in some regards, but was wildly neglectful in others. June took it upon herself to raise us and turn us into acceptable ladies. Looking back, I've always thought our growing up years pleasant, but now, I see that we were never told anything about our parents' family. I have a distant memory of a long hall filled with portraits of our family going back through the years. But I know of no other details." She sighed. "When Uncle died, we were told that our new home was in a small cottage here in Brighton. Then we were told that the whole of it had been passed off to another distant cousin to Uncle, The Duke of Granbury." She smiled. "And then to Morley himself, in a game of cards."

"That is true?" Julia shook her head. "I saw something about it in *Whims and Fancies*, but hardly believed such a thing."

"Too true. It made for some difficult conversations between June and Morley, but all is well now. You can perhaps understand how any news that the Standish name is not a lost and lonely family is welcome to my identity and lost soul." Kate laughed. "Do I sound overly dramatic, I wonder?"

"You have just the proper response. And what do you know so far about the connection of the castle to your family?" Logan had become intently interested in their quest to know more of her family.

"If the ties are accurate, and we are related to William the Conqueror himself, which I'm pretty certain, then the castle could very well have been built for the female descendants of

William. He said so in a letter we found deep in the wall of the castle."

"This is incredible. You have such a thing?" Julia leaned forward.

"We do. When you come for dinner, perhaps we can take it out to show you. He wrote that he hoped his daughters would always have a home."

"So intriguing." Logan nodded, watching her. To think of her past few years, he could understand they were difficult indeed.

"I suppose it has been useful to us to be distantly royal. Members of the ton have helped us to have clothing and extra food baskets. We used to have many a visitor at our small cottage. It sat directly off the road as one would enter Brighton from London."

"But you felt lost and unlinked to anyone." He wanted to reach for her hand.

Kate's eyes widened. "Yes. That's exactly how I feel."

"Even now."

"Somewhat, I suppose."

From the rigid manner in which she held herself in this moment, Logan would guess that she was still powerfully influenced by her insecurity about where she truly belonged.

"Lucy is even more driven. She feels it her duty to bring respectability back to the line. She thinks we should all marry for title only." Kate laughed. "We tease her for it."

"But you understand." Julia's eyes were filled with sympathy.

"I do." Kate toyed with her plate. "My concerns are not so much with title or recognition. I would greatly like to be grounded into a family, to be tied to them as though a long, invisible string connected us to our past."

"There's more."

Kate nodded. "And I never . . ." She looked at them both. "Never want to be hungry again."

"Oh, you poor dear!" Julia moved around the table to squeeze Kate across the shoulders.

"And perhaps this is frivolous." Kate's eyes flitted to Logan's and then away. "But I never want to wear last year's fashions again, either."

Logan laughed. "This, I see." Perhaps he'd stumbled upon part of the reason for her unhappiness. "No chance of that now. You seem to create the latest fashions. You're on the cusp of them all the time." He dipped his head. "I would venture to say you have a gift in this area."

"A gift of a frivolous waste?" Kate's eyebrows rose in challenge.

"Oh that I could rid that moment from your memory. My fashion exploits are a widely abused, distractive, frivolous use of my time and energy. Yours are a work of art."

"Oh now, no. Yours are equally a work of art. I would like to see the infamous cravat again sometime. I hope you haven't cowered in fear at your opponents . . ." The challenge in her eyes amused him and sparked a bit of an idea. "I will. If you create something equally bold."

"Done. I will do so. And we will wear them together."

Logan held out a hand. "Let's shake on it, as Julia is our witness."

Her hand in his caused his feelings to surge again, and he wanted more than anything to stand, pull her into his arms, and kiss away any insecurities she had remaining. But instead, he just winked. "When shall we do such a thing?"

"It must be in the most public of places." Kate lifted her chin in challenge.

"Prinny's ball." Logan laughed at the most perfectness of the suggestion.

"Most excellent." Kate tapped a finger on her chin. "I will have to work on my plan."

Julia looked from one to the other. "I do believe you two are a force alone. Together, no one will be able to keep up."

As Logan studied Kate's responding laugh, he knew his sister to be exactly right.

Chapter Fourteen

⚜

Kate hurried back into the castle with the history book clutched under her arm. She had vowed to be the utmost careful with such a precious volume. She went straight for the library, then their family sitting room, then the front rooms. Not seeing anyone, anywhere, she hurried up the stairs and placed the book carefully on her dressing table. Then she went in search of a servant, someone who would know where everyone had gone.

Sniffling sounds distracted her once she exited out into the family wing hall. She followed the sound and found Lucy, alone in her room, wiping her eyes.

"Oh, Lucy." Kate ran to her sister. "What is it? What has happened"

Lucy's eyes widened in surprise. "I thought I was alone. I'm sorry to distress you."

Kate wrapped her arms around Lucy's small shoulders. "Tell me."

"Oh, there's nothing to tell." Lucy tried to wave her away.

But Kate pulled up her other chair and sat close, pulling

Lucy's hand into her own. "Please. What is distressing you? I can't bear to see this sadness."

Lucy's sigh was quiet but long. "I just . . ." She shook her head. "I don't know what to do about Lord Tanner."

Kate was surprised at this response. "Is there something to be done? Have things progressed between you?"

"Not really, no. But they could. I think I could encourage things to progress, you know, how some ladies do."

Kate thought of her moments on the beach. She would die before she told her sisters of her brazen behavior. "Yes. You mean, like smile, and give him attention, flirt with him?"

"Yes. Yes, those things. But . . ." She turned to Kate. "I find I abhor the man."

Not expecting anything of the like from her sister, Kate sat back and laughed. "Well, then what is the problem?"

"The problem? He's the only available almost duke in the ton right now. And I can't find a way to like him."

Kate shook her head. "No. You cannot be thinking you must live with a man you abhor simply because he will be a duke."

"But Kate, don't you see? Our family deserves this. We were meant to be those with titles. We were meant to be part of the royal court."

"With Henry I. Come, Lucy. We don't need to be a part of this royal court. You wish to be related to the Hanover lines? To Charlotte and . . . Prinny?" Kate made a face, which brought out the hoped for laugh in Lucy.

"Most definitely not. But I do so hope to have a Standish bloodline sit as a duke." Lucy's shoulders drooped. "But I haven't as yet been able to stomach him."

Kate's laugh shook her belly. "Then I say desist with this plan. There are plenty of other reasons to marry. And we have an earl. That's enough titling for all of us." She thought immediately of Lord Dennison. Marquess. And wondered if Lucy would be at ease were Kate to marry a marquess. Marry Lord Dennison? She'd of course given him all of her thoughts since their kiss, and the idea of spending the rest of her life with such a man would be such a pleasure. Her joy would be full, she was sure of it.

But would he want her if he knew of her connection to *Her Lady's Whims and Fancies*? Would she have a need for this income if she were married to him?

"Do you ever worry about food and money and providing for ourselves?" Kate asked.

"All the time."

"And if our husbands should die? What then?"

"Yes. I worry about that, too."

Kate knew that the concern would never leave her. She knew what happened when people died—everyone they cared about was left destitute. They had lived that very nightmare for too long for Kate to ever forget or lose the fear that one day she or her children might be left in the same situation. As ashamed as she was about her *Whims and Fancies* work, she couldn't regret it for that reason alone. She was building some kind of manner in which to provide for herself.

She squeezed Lucy. "I've got some good news. Let me run to grab something." By the time she was back, Grace had joined Lucy in her room.

"Where's Charity?" Kate asked.

"She's coming," Grace replied.

"Excellent. I have something to show you." Kate held up the book.

Grace wrinkled her nose. "An old book?"

"Oh, stop. You are going to love this. I promise."

Charity at last joined them with a flourish and landed on the bed first.

Kate followed and climbed up on Lucy's bed. The others

joined her, and for a moment, Kate just smiled at them all. "Just missing June." The nostalgia hit pretty hard, but she grinned through it. "I love us, dear sisters."

"Yes, I love us, too." Grace reached her arms out as wide as she could and got up on her knees, scooting closer.

They all collapsed together in a tangle of arms and shoulders and skirts. Then fell back in a fit of laughter. Kate felt a few of the broken pieces caused by her worries close up and heal. The world shifted closer to where it should be. Then she sat back against the headboard and opened up the book. "This is a history of Brighton, and more particularly, a history of this very castle."

"Ooh." Grace moved to sit at her side. "You're right, I will like this one."

Kate read to them the connection with William the Conqueror, why he had the castle built, and who lived there, and then read them one particularly powerful paragraph.

". . . William was known to have touted many times that this castle was for his wife, for his daughters. The women in his family were to benefit. And although marauders and even greedy male members of his family tried to take it for their own, he zealously defended its walls, declaring, "It is for my Matilda and her daughters or no one at all.""

Kate felt happy gooseflesh prickle up and down her arms. "That is us."

"But how do we know for certain?" Charity pursed her lips. "I would like to believe that as much as anyone, but how do we know?"

"We don't, but we are working on it."

"We?"

"Oh. Lord Dennison. This is his book."

"Lord Dennison." Charity grinned.

"Yes, but that's beside the point." She showed them the

genealogy page and the empty space. "There are a few theories that this is Matilda. Right here in this line. And I wonder if we aren't related through her line."

"But I thought we were related through Henry I."

"We are as well. But a more direct connection might be found through Matilda. And if through her, then this castle really would well and truly belong to us."

"And any other of her direct descendants."

"True." Kate frowned. "And really, to Morley now, and June, so what does it matter?" She puffed out a breath. "But it does matter. I want to know where we come from."

"So do I." Charity nodded her head.

Kate leaned her head back. "Who remembers Mother and Father?"

They settled onto the bed, each one knowing where this conversation would go. June, who remembered the most, was not present, of course, but they all had memories to share.

"I'll go first." Grace leaned her head on Kate's shoulder.

As they went through the stories they each remembered of their parents, Kate grasped onto the knowledge of who they were and where they came from, and settled into the familiar feelings of love they shared.

Charity adjusted her legs beneath her. "I had another memory come to me last night, something I haven't thought of in years."

"What was it?" Grace leaned forward.

"Mother. She led me down a long portrait gallery. She stopped in front of one, a woman."

Kate sucked in her breath, waiting for more, but Charity stopped. "What did she say? Who was it?"

"I don't know. I don't remember. Just that feeling of being a part of something special." She frowned. "I tried to fall back to sleep to see the rest of the dream, but it was gone."

"What if it was Matilda?" Kate asked

"Would they have a portrait that old?"

Kate shook her head, not sure of anything. "I found some old clothes."

Charity wrinkled her nose. "I'm not wearing them."

Everyone laughed.

"Of course, not. But they might have clues."

Grace stretched. "I say we talk about this tomorrow."

"Yes, me, too." Lucy smiled at Kate.

They all made their way out of Lucy's room, Kate last of all. "Thanks for our chat today."

"No, I thank you. Talking with everyone helped me remember who I am. A Standish daughter cannot just marry anyone, duke or no."

"That's right. One thing I know for sure. There aren't many men in the world who deserve you."

"You either, sister. Is this Lord Dennison someone who would make you happy?"

Kate couldn't stop her smile. "I think so."

"Then I wish you the very best."

Kate held up a hand. "Don't be wishing me well quite yet. I want to know much more about him before I decide any well-wishing would be necessary."

"I'd like to talk to him as well."

"I wish you would. Ask him anything you can think of."

She laughed. "I will. And I pity him if Charity gets ahold of him."

"I don't even know if he's a Whig or a Tory."

"As if such a thing matters in marriage."

"It would matter to Charity."

"Yes, it would."

Kate hugged Lucy. "Goodnight, sister."

Kate found easy sleep that night, with thoughts of her

family line and Lord Dennison making her smile all the way into her dreams.

The next day found her early in the library, sending off the plates and a new article for *Whims and Fancies*, one that spoke of a fashionable lord who found a way to present himself in the most classic manner possible. She hoped to turn the tide of the comments spoken about Lord Dennison. She drew plates of the fashions she would be wearing the next week as well, and then sent them all off through a footman.

Then she found her way to the old part of the castle, to begin digging through crates of clothing. She sifted through the oldest fabrics, some falling apart in her fingers, then she pulled out what looked like a small chest. "What is this?" Her fingers trembled as she lifted the chest and placed it in her lap. She adjusted the latch and then lifted the cover. "Oh." The precious items inside gave her the feeling of opening a window into history—into her family? Perhaps. She lifted out a small rattle, a child's toy, solid gold. It felt heavy in her hand. The handle was engraved with the initials MMS. Could this be it? She sifted through the other items, most falling into dust. Then another small pouch, the leather soft but still intact, caught her eye. She lifted it, pouring something heavy into her hand.

A ring. A small signet ring that looked to fit a woman. Kate didn't recognize the coat of arms, but inside, somewhat worn, was one word, a name. She almost jumped up excitedly. Matilda.

King William's wife's name was Matilda. But the fact that this ring rested in a chest with a baby rattle meant something, perhaps. She carefully closed the chest and latched it, clutching the rattle and ring in her hand. She moved swiftly through the castle to find her sisters. Perhaps she'd need to get them out of their beds, but no matter. She also sought the book. Perhaps there would be more to learn in the book about Queen Matilda.

Chapter Fifteen

A week full of lovely encounters with Kate—both planned and unplanned—followed, leading to tonight's familial dinner with the Standishes. Logan and Julia stood at the front door of the castle. He straightened his jacket with a smile.

"Are you wearing that pink monstrosity for a reason?"

He stood taller. "Do you not like it?"

"I've told you before what I think of it."

"But I haven't changed your mind, even with all my handsome smiles and charming personality?"

"It's been weeks since you've worn your more colorful pieces. And that cravat. The Croatian knot has returned. Are you sure you're well?"

"I'm perfectly well. What could possibly be wrong with me?"

The door opened to the Standishes' butler, with Miss Kate right behind, wearing the largest headdress Logan had ever seen. He stopped his laugh, but only just, and kept a straight face as he bowed over her hand. "That's a lovely pair of feathers." The two largest plumes rose high above her head.

"Why, thank you. The peacock who donated them will feel gratified to know, I'm certain." Kate put her hands around his arm and smiled at Julia. "I'm so pleased you could come."

"I as well, though now, I'm feeling slightly underdressed."

"I have extra feathers if you'd like."

"Only if you also have an extra very pink jacket."

"Unfortunately, I think that jacket is an original," Kate said.

'Of course, it's an original. Do I appear in society with anything copied or fake? Have I ever?" Logan replied.

"No, no, brother. We would never sincerely suspect you of such a thing."

"Just so." He entered the Standish castle with his two favorite women on his arms. "I have good feelings about this dinner. Thank you for having us, Miss Kate."

The Duke of Granbury entered the main hall. "We're pleased you could come."

The duchess entered at his side. "Yes, this is lovely."

"You've outdone yourself, Dennison, and just when *Her Lady's Whims and Fancies* has mentioned your new, more classical look."

"What's this?" Could the *Whims and Fancies* writers be following him around?

"Perhaps they took note of your appearance at the assembly ball." Julia squeezed his arm, knowing how much it meant to him to be viewed in a more serious and dedicated light.

Kate knew as well, but she was strangely stiff at his side.

He looked down at the top of her head. She must have felt his gaze. When she looked up at him, he winked.

Her smile grew, and then she nodded. "It's just as it should be. I'm happy they are appreciating your finer qualities."

The duke led them into the sisters' large dining room. "We

don't stand much on ceremony here. Please come in and sit where you like. The others will join us."

Kate laughed beside him. "I don't know what's come over him."

Then his two boys entered the room, their infant in the hands of the nurse and their young chap walking sedately with jacket, cravat, and breeches.

"What's this?" Kate ran to him. "You are looking very fine, my lord." She curtseyed.

And then the lad performed the most perfect bow Logan had seen a lad do.

"Would you look at that." Logan grinned at the lad, obviously enjoying his display of exceptional manners.

Soon, the room was full of chattering sisters, his own as well as the Standishes, with the occasional deeper voice sounding a response from himself or His Grace. And Logan loved every minute. At one point, amidst happy chatter and laughter all around the table of all energy levels, His Grace and Logan shared a gaze. The duke's eyes sparkled with joy, and he reached for his wife's hand. Logan knew this was what he wanted—this family, this love, this trust between two people. His gaze moved to Kate's, who was wiping laughter tears from her eyes, and he knew. The more he came to know this beautiful woman, the more certain he became of their potential happiness together. Now, to be sure she felt the same, that she would be equally engaged, that she would accept his suit. He grimaced inside. A rejection from Kate would do far more to his heart than the mere tearing that Olivia had inflicted. A rejection from Kate would shred his inner organ from his body and deposit it elsewhere forever.

He forced a swallow of his wine and tried to smile.

"You look as though your impending death had suddenly come calling," Julia leaned closer and murmured in his ear.

He forced another smile. "Better?"

She laughed. "Worse. What's come over you?"

"Just my constant fears and insecurities coming to plague me."

A servant brought in a tray with papers.

Lucy waved the footman over. "Oh, excellent. I wanted to share something I read that sounds frightfully familiar."

"Lucy, I wonder if now is not the time?"

Kate's sister just shook her head, all smiles. "These are too good not to share. To think, sisters, we are famous."

When Miss Lucy held up the paper, Logan groaned. She'd be sharing *Her Lady's Whims and Fancies.* He braced himself. Julia's hand rested on his arm.

Lucy read, "Our king of masterful, though overdone, cravats has perhaps had a transformation. I know our readers will be shocked to hear he has been seen twice in one week wearing black, a simple Oriental knot, and speaking of, you will be amazed to hear, his upcoming work in the House of Lords." Lucy lifted her eyes and laughed. "Do you see that?" She kept reading. "On the contrary, a young family of sisters has taken Brighton and their castle by storm. Their dress is as garish as it is tasteful. They are to be sought for fashion advice, as they seem to wear the latest before we even hear of it." Lucy laughed again. "Did you hear that? That's all because of you, Kate!"

"Wh-what?"

"You keep us dressed and with hair styled the way you do. Someone has noticed, and now we're famous."

"Not exactly what I hoped to become famous for." Charity took a sip of her drink.

"There's more."

"More?" Kate's surprise seemed genuine. Why wouldn't there be more?

"Someone has written a counter assessment."

Kate jumped to her feet. "Let me see that." She stood over Lucy's shoulder, and after a glance, shook her head. "This cannot be."

She reached for it, but Lucy held it away. "Come now, this is good entertainment."

Kate shared a long look with Lucy for a moment, and then Lucy shrugged. "Or if you want, we can put it away."

"Thank you. Nothing more to see in that article. How wonderful that we are all featured so positively."

"How odd." Julia's gaze flit from Kate, who had returned to her seat, to Lucy and back.

"I'll not complain if they never read it again," Logan said.

Their conversation was held as quiet murmurs to each other. "I quite agree with you."

Kate had returned to her seat, and conversations were resuming, but Kate had not looked up from her hands. Logan guessed she was reading the papers.

When dinner was at last finished and everyone had moved to a sitting room, Lucy moved to the piano forte to play, and Logan approached Kate. "What did the paper say?"

"Pardon?" She jumped. "Oh." She looked away. "It was nothing."

"Kate, you don't think I will see it? We probably have a copy at the house."

"Oh, you're so right. I just didn't want to interrupt the mood at dinner, and I didn't want it to be a group discussion. But I am shocked at what they did."

"Might I see it?"

Kate looked around the room and then sighed. "Very well. Come with me."

He followed her through two more rooms and then into what looked like a library. "You have a lovely collection, too."

"Some are very old. We found them in a room full of crates."

"Did you search more through the clothing?"

"Oh, I did. I cannot wait to show you. We found a baby rattle. And a signet ring!"

"Did you recognize the crest?"

"Not yet. We need to match it, but I suspect it to be William's wife, or their daughter, with the name of Matilda." She led him partway into the room.

A messy and crowded-looking desk sat at one end of the room, and another table with chairs at the other. She made her way to the table and lifted the papers. "Come, let's go talk on the outside verandah."

"Why not in here? I like this room. We could explore your book collection as we did mine . . ." Logan stepped closer and lifted her hand to his mouth.

"We've been in here too long alone as it is. I don't wish to abuse the duke's kindness in his giving us so much freedom, nor do I wish to disappoint June or Morley by causing trouble."

"Who would even consider this scandalous in our present group? Your sisters? Mine?"

"The servants?" Kate raised one brow.

"And you feel they would consider it newsworthy enough to spread our clandestine meeting in an old library to all in Brighton?"

"I can only guess. When you see *Whims*, you might wonder how people get their information. I certainly do." Her frown grew. "Oh, read it already."

He lifted and unfolded the paper. Then he read aloud, "Contrary to the belief of some who might feel that a certain lord has made a complete transformation into a well-thinking, hard-working marquess, he is just biding his time. He will woo us all, and then at the most opportune moment, don the jester's outfit once more and make fools of us all."

Logan was surprised at his own inner turmoil. The words,

though meant to be humorous, were as hurtful as any he'd read, and they tore at his ability to make a difference. Who would ever take him seriously if the attention continued?

"Why would someone do this? How do they know or care about my efforts for the House of Lords?" He shook his head in quiet disbelief.

"I'm sorry." Kate's voice, a half-strangled whisper, shook him out of his selfish, encompassing focus.

Her face was pained, almost panicked, and her hands shook.

"No, no. Come here. Please don't be so unhappy." He pulled her close and wrapped his arms around her. "This has to go away sometime. I'll be fine. As long as I don't wear this pink jacket in public again . . ." He laughed. But she didn't respond.

He pulled away to get a good look at her face. She looked determined, stoic. She lifted her chin. "I have to tell you something." Then her lip trembled.

Logan's hand went to the side of her face; tenderly, gently, his thumb caressed the soft skin near her mouth, hoping to tug it upward.

When she lifted her eyes to his, there was so much desperation or something in them, so much worry, that he pressed his lips to hers. It was meant to be a quick, soft motion to set her mind at ease, but her response was anything but soft. She clung to him, her kisses almost fierce in their intensity, the longing obvious, the pleading for . . . something. She tugged and kissed, and when her teeth bit into his lower lip, he was lost. One tiny thread of awareness reminded him where they were, but his arms pulled her closer. He leaned back against the edge of the table, pulling her even closer, and responded to every bit of her urgency with increasing tension of his own.

Until someone cleared their throat in the doorway. His foggy mind only half-registered the noise. "I was just looking for something to read . . ." The Duke of Granbury's voice sounded anything but amused.

Logan paused, resting his mouth against Kate's to give her a moment, then turned to His Grace. He tried humor. With the corner of his mouth raised, he laughed. "That was our intent as well."

But the duke did not smile. His stare bore into Logan with the protectivity of an angry father, and Logan knew his place. As his arms pulled Kate close one more time and he kissed her forehead, he murmured, "Why don't you let me talk to the duke for a moment?"

She looked away and nodded, and then ran from the room.

Chapter Sixteen

K ate half-sobbed, half-moaned all the way to June's room. Even though June was not home, she needed her. She needed some good advice, something, anything, and so she fell on her oldest sister's bed and cried out her guilt. For that was the strongest feeling to rule the moment. Guilt that she had created such a problem for Lord Dennison, one she hadn't been able to fix simply by writing a complimentary report. And she wanted to tell him. Would he still love her? Or would he think she had betrayed him and hate her like he did Olivia? Could she give him up for the sake of being honest?

If she couldn't look him in the face without the cloud of guilt taking over her peace, what was the point of being together?

A soft hand rested on her shoulder.

Kate turned.

Amelia sat beside her on the bed. "It's not so very awful, is it? To be kissing the man that you love?" Her eyes sparkled with fun. "We should celebrate another upcoming wedding, no?"

Kate's eyes widened. "What do you mean?" Her mind raced

to their kiss and Gerald's angry expression. "No. Amelia. No. We cannot be forced to marry."

"Forced isn't precisely the word, but I do believe neither of you has a choice."

"Of course, we do. We are here in my home with only family around. No one here need force us."

Amelia's soft hands took Kate's in her own. "It is not merely a matter of reputation. If you are finding moments alone in such an intense manner, it is best you marry now, and then you won't need to try and avoid each other."

Kate tried to understand her words, but knew she was missing a rather large something, and she suspected it had more to do with married women than she would be able to grasp now. "That is ridiculous. As if Lord Dennison and I could not be alone together without behaving . . . When are we ever alone, anyway?" Often, if she were being honest. And every time, they had found a moment to kiss. Two times. "We can easily continue a . . . courtship, without behaving . . . Oh, Amelia. This might ruin everything."

"I'm more concerned about a different kind of ruin. Gerald asked me to speak to you. He said Lord Dennison is willing to do his duty by you. He is an honorable man. Who I think you love . . . You do love him, don't you?"

"Painfully so."

Amelia's worry lines relaxed. "Then I see no problem here at all." She ran her fingers through Kate's hair, pulling out pins one by one. "You two shall be very happy together. And a marquess. Do you think Lucy will approve?" Amelia's laugh should have brought a smile to Kate's face, but she could only feel a rising sense of dread.

"He has gone home to find a ring, to get his papers in order, and then he will return to talk over the contracts with Gerald. I expect he will propose if that meeting ends to everybody's satisfaction."

Kate shook her head. "This is . . . nothing like I had imagined." She thought of Lord Dennison, forced into proposing before he was ready, thought of the fear that must be going through his mind, thought of her great betrayal of him. "Oh, Amelia. I've done something just awful. Once he finds out, he won't want to marry me." The words came out as though forced. If they had stayed inside any longer, perhaps she would have burst.

"What are you talking about?" Amelia's face then cleared in recognition. "Oh, your fashion plates?"

"I knew you knew."

"How could I not? I'd recognize your work anywhere."

"No one else knows."

"Knows what?" Charity stood in the doorway, with Lucy and Grace crowding in beside her.

Kate waved them in. "You may as well all know. I'm in a terrible bind."

Amelia laughed. "Oh, I don't think you're in a bind at all, nor is it terrible."

They all gathered in close on the bed; Kate leaned back against the headboard. "Lord Dennison is going to propose."

Their happy squeals and bouncing on the bed made Kate smile. For a moment, she responded as though the news was such that deserved well-wishing. She received their hugs and laughed in a bouncing, girly celebration. But then, she shook her head.

"You don't seem as happy as I would have thought." Charity looked from Amelia to Kate and back.

"We were caught . . . in the library."

"Caught?" Grace's eyes widened.

Lucy gasped, and Charity looked like she wanted to laugh

out loud.

Kate felt much worse about her words in *Whims and Fancies* than being caught kissing Lord Dennison, but they could think what they would for a moment. All would be told. "You are going to think me the worst sort of person."

Charity studied her face. "For what?"

She sighed. "All that time spent eating turnips and relying on the goodness of others for our well-being? I just can't ever do that again."

"Who says you will have to? Things are better now." Grace's concerned frown made Kate wish to protect her from her own worries, but she had to tell someone what she'd done.

"I started to work."

"Work?"

"Yes, I submit things to the *Morning Star* paper, and they print them, and I get paid."

No one said anything for a long enough time that Kate started to feel uncomfortable. Then Charity nodded. *"Her Lady's Whims and Fancies?* That's you?"

The others gasped again.

"Oh, you don't have to be so horrified."

"But Lord Dennison." Lucy shook her head. "And today, at dinner. I'm sorry."

"It's not your fault. How could you know?"

"Why didn't you tell us?"

"I didn't know if it would come to anything. I still don't make enough to support anyone, not even myself, but I thought I could make it grow."

They sat in silence again.

"Think about it. People die. No provisions are made for us. And we are cast off."

"But I know our parents had to have made provisions." Lucy had always said so, no matter so much evidence to the contrary.

"We've talked about this before. And how would we ever know? The estate is with whatever cousin inherited the entail, and we were put in the care of Uncle." Charity frowned.

"Who died." Kate grimaced. "I don't mean to sound morose, but haven't we learned that nothing about our care is certain? Things happen. Mistakes, careless things, even selfish things. And I . . . I am afraid." She hugged her knees, realizing for the first time how deep-rooted were her fears. "I can't . . . I can't go hungry again."

Grace moved closer and put her head on Kate's shoulder. The others' moods were somber.

Lucy rested a soft hand on Kate's arm. "But if you marry Lord Dennison, you will be a marchioness. Surely, that comes with it certain assurances."

"Not to mention your dowry, and when Gerald works out the marriage settlement, he will ensure you are cared for, including in the will in case of Lord Dennison's untimely death," Amelia said.

Kate nodded. "You can do that?"

"Certainly." Amelia squeezed her hand.

A portion of her angst lessoned. "So I only need continue at *The Morning Star* if I wish to?"

"Sounds like it to me," Amelia said.

"And I will, of course, care for each one of you," Kate told her sisters. "June will as well, and we will have this castle." She felt all the knots in her body begin to loosen. But then she dropped her head to her knees. "I have to tell Lord Dennison. He must know. From me, before he discovers I've written about him."

"What is he going to think?" Amelia's question burned inside Kate as one she most desperatey wished to know.

"He might not want to marry me once he finds out. He really wants to be able to trust his wife . . ." She sighed. "It is the worst possible quandary. "And he's attempting to do good, for tenants. He has a possible law he's written and everything, which would help protect tenants."

"Is such a thing popular with the House of Lords?" Charity's skepticism did not surprise Kate.

"You know it's not, but he is not without friends. A group from Oxford, but they might not take him seriously. He's been such a fashion paragon for so long, it does put him at a disadvantage among those whose respect he would hope to win."

"What if you start a whole new campaign before you quit? What if you divert their attention? Focus on some other than his being a fashion paragon?" Lucy's calculating expression had everyone on the bed leaning closer.

Lucy sat taller, bolt upright. "What if . . . you create a fictional person who is even more outlandish than Lord Dennison ever was—a competition to Brummel himself? And write about him. Place him far away from here, put him in Bath. Perhaps they'll leave well enough alone with our dear Dennison."

Lucy's idea brought such a sense of hope, Kate smiled. "And perhaps I won't have to tell him at all?"

The others looked away. Amelia shook her head. "You should tell him."

She closed her eyes. "I suppose." But inside, she wondered if she could divert the attention well enough, if there wouldn't even be a need to explain she'd been the creator of *Whims and Fancies*, and then she could set it aside and perhaps write other things? Her mind spun with possibilities and the hope that all in her life was not in fact lost, making her heart flutter with light. Her smile began weakly, felt wavery, but it grew. "Thank you, sisters. What would we do without each other?"

They folded in toward each other again, Amelia as well, and their hugs and tears were a balm to Kate's hurting heart. When they pulled apart, Kate laughed. "Who'd have thought I'd be forced to marry." She sniffed, indignation rising. "In fact, I'm not okay with that." She crossed her arms.

"What do you mean?" Amelia studied her face.

"Who wants a man that had to be forced to marry them?" She looked from each sister to the other. And no one seemed to have an answer.

"What if I say no?"

"He might be sad . . ." Grace's kind eyes gave Kate pause.

But she waved her hands. "No, what if I say no, and then we continue on as before until we're ready to take that step?"

"Again. He might be sad." Lucy's expression was intent.

"I wouldn't advise such a thing. Or at least talk it through with him. Perhaps in the same conversation where you let him know about *Whims and Fancies?*" Amelia's voice was gentle, but the more Kate thought about her options, the more disgruntled she became.

"Why does it even matter? We are family. All of you know I'm not ruined. We wouldn't tell a soul. I feel that we are free to act."

No one seemed to agree with her. Even Charity's expression was concerned, and Amelia smiled her gentle, but suddenly now aggravating, smile. "We've talked about this. There is more to it than that."

Kate sighed. "I know. It's just not a good situation to be in, is it?"

"Talk to him. You two can figure this out."

Kate nodded, but she couldn't admit that a part of her hoped that she would be able to fix the *Whims and Fancies* situation enough that Lord Dennison would never know she'd done such a thing. The other part of her knew she'd only rid herself of this awful guilt if she confessed, accepting the consequences even if he were mad at her forever.

Chapter Seventeen

Logan shook hands with His Grace. "I'm not just doing my duty by her. She is the choice of my heart. I love Miss Kate."

"And what about the disrespect I saw happening right in her own home?"

"Disrespect? That was not disrespect. That was my heart speaking to her heart."

The duke's eyebrow rose.

"And a little bit of me not being able to resist such a beautiful woman, but Your Grace, sir, I love her, and like I said, I'm happy to ask her to marry me right now." Logan couldn't dim his smile, even though he knew he must look like a simpleton smiling so large at the duke. But it couldn't be helped. He was happy. He loved Kate. And she loved him. He could tell. No woman would kiss him like that if she didn't love him. With just that one moment, she'd wiped out any worry of her ever turning him down, any worry that she might not return his love. She was all in. Even if she'd never said it with her words, she'd said it with her lips, and he'd never been happier.

"You know, she might not be happy about this situation."

He shook his head. "No, she's happy all right."

The duke smiled. "I'm not saying she doesn't want to marry you. I'm saying, she might not like the idea of you being forced to do so." He straightened his jacket. "So, I'm not forcing you. You do what you want to make this right. And to keep her happy. You need to talk to her."

"She's happy about it. I—I can tell."

"She ran from the room."

He was about to counter with something, anything else, but then he considered. The duke was right. Why had she run from the room? "Is she unhappy about this?"

"I think it might be embarrassing. And I'll just give you one bit of advice. Every woman wants to know she's the choice of your heart."

"How could she not know that?"

"Just make sure she does."

The next day, Logan and Julia were once again sitting together in the library. She'd already chastised him for kissing Miss Kate, and then squealed in happiness that he was going to get married. And now they read lazily, each in their favorite chair.

A footman came in bearing a tray. "We have received some correspondence."

"Very good. I'll take it here," Logan said.

He handed Julia her letters and then tapped on one of his own. "A card from the prince."

"Oh?" Julia only half-heard. She looked to be deep in a letter.

Logan opened it. "The prince is having another ball."

"Hmm."

"He wants me to come wearing a new cravat. And he wants to know the knot beforehand so that he might wear it, too."

She put down her letter. "That's quite a statement."

"I know." Logan read it again. "He's inviting a core set of us to attend with him." He tapped the card again. "This could be a good thing."

"It's definitely great for your new cravat. Is it good for your new bill? Your goals?"

"I think so." Logan stood. "How could it not be? Prinny is what Prinny is, but he also has great influence. If he came forward in support of anything—my bill, for example—that would have sway." He paced. "My . . . popularity could have a good use after all. I've attracted the prince's attention. And now he . . . he wants to be seen wearing one of my original cravats . . . How much time do we have? This much be a masterpiece." He hurried to leave the room. "I must call Wiggins. We have to get started. It must be stupendous!"

Julia laughed. "I can't wait to read *Her Lady's Whims and Fancies*."

"I think the prince can't, either. He hasn't been the subject in that column for weeks." He stepped out of the room and asked the nearest maid to call for his valet.

Later, Logan put down his sketching materials. He and Wiggins had finally come up with something spectacular. "Ensure that if we use any printed cloths, that the prince has the same print. We have but a week, and must not waste a moment."

"Very good, my lord. I will obtain the necessary items. And might I ask, could we begin practice tomorrow?"

"This evening."

The valet nodded. Then Logan sat at his desk and pulled out a paper and quill. "I must respond to the prince." Once finished with a lavish and complimentary response, he pulled out a new sheaf. "My Dearest Kate." One benefit to being caught in a compromising situation was that they were almost engaged, and no one would think twice to his sending a letter.

Once finished with his letter, Logan gave a servant instructions as to its delivery and which flowers to send, and then he descended the stairs to meet with his tailor. They had work to do, and the man would faint in ridiculous ecstasy when he heard of this next jacket's use, and then he might faint in worry when he learned that Logan needed it in one week's time.

But it couldn't be helped. The ball was the perfect reason to have a new jacket. In truth, it would be an insult to His Highness for Logan to show up with something he'd worn somewhere else.

THE SISTERS ALL GATHERED AROUND KATE'S DESK.

"So this is where you design all those plates?" Lucy sifted through her papers. "These are magnificent." She ran her finger along a sketch of a new turban Kate was working on. "I would love to wear this."

"You could."

"Do I dare? It is such a statement piece."

"Certainly, you dare. There's nothing to it."

"Back to our purpose. For our imaginary distraction, we must create something even more ostentatious." Charity flipped through the cards that Kate had already created. "I can't believe I'm saying this. What if he were to create a brand new cravat and had a jacket to go along with it?"

"What do you mean?"

"Something new, bold, never done before in the design? And a color that's never worn."

"Yes, I agree. But I would need to be vague about the details of the cravat. I don't know enough about them . . ." They all shared a look. "And yes, I know Lord Dennison knows, but we cannot tell him."

Charity's continued stare forced Kate to say, "Yet."

"Fine. How about a new cut? Can you guess in what direction the cuts of men's jackets are going and pre-empt the next phase? Aren't they getting shorter around here?" Charity indicated her midsection. "With a vest, like Lord Ballustrade?"

Kate nodded at her sister. "You could be the next author of *Her Lady's Whims and Fancies.*"

"No, thank you. Not unless the editor allows me to print my opinions about some of the new laws Parliament is trying to create."

Kate considered her sister. "Not entirely what they're looking for, but you've caused me to think more in this light; I wonder if there's a way to mention it in a palatable manner."

"Only you would know about that." Charity said the obvious.

"So what if we also describe his hair? Something entirely different from what Lord Dennison usually does."

"And a different color." Lucy nodded.

Grace giggled. "Feathers. Can he wear feathers?"

"Yes, with a cap or something, right here." Lucy indicated that it should sit at an angle.

"Oh, that's most excellent." Kate tapped her quill on the end of her chin. "Breeches."

The sisters smiled. Lucy shook her head. "Do you dare?"

"Of course, I dare. A woman can mention breeches without blushing." She felt her own cheeks warm. "Though I seem to find it impossible."

They laughed, and Kate sketched. She wondered why she hadn't involved her sisters from the very first moment. Success or failure, the whole experience was better with them involved.

Once they'd decided on the man's new look, Kate was

pleased. "This is more genius than we realized. It really is the direction fashion is moving. I wouldn't be surprised to see more men dress like this, with or without *Whims and Fancies*."

A servant stepped into the library carrying a very large vase full of fresh flowers. "A delivery for Miss Kate."

"Thank you. Please set them on that table there. And Finnis, could you send this express? To London?"

"Yes, miss. Very good." He bowed and took their new gossip out of the room.

"Well, it's done, then."

Kate moved to the flowers.

"Those are so beautiful." Grace looked like she wanted to swoon herself.

Kate laughed. "They're from Lord Dennison." She lifted a paper, sealed with his signet. She ran her finger over the hardened wax. "I do love his coat of arms." The sisters gathered round. A tall horse up on its hind legs faced a large cat. Two swords crossed in the middle.

"Oh come, we aren't going to get anything out of Kate until she reads her letter."

"Wait, what's this?" Lucy lifted another letter Kate hadn't noticed. "It's from the Royal Pavilion! Prince George." She broke the seal immediately. "A ball. We're invited to be a part of his special consort at the ball in one week's time." Her eyes shining, she grinned at Kate. "I think we can thank you for this."

"Perhaps, Lord Dennison." Kate stepped away.

Charity turned to go. "We can discuss our clothes for the ball tomorrow. I've had enough fashion to last me . . . probably forever."

Kate hardly heard as they faced away. She lowered herself into her most comfortable chair and broke the seal.

My Dearest Kate,

With great sadness, I must go about my next few days without seeing you. But I console myself knowing that we will both be at the ball. Prepare yourself—the prince has dictated our clothing choices, and I will have several surprises that I hope you of all people will appreciate. I know we have much to discuss, and I long to do so. At the duke's request, I will go to my solicitor this afternoon, and hope to talk more with you when I have the particulars.

WHILE I KNOW SOME MIGHT CONSIDER OUR ACTIONS *regrettable, I cannot find them so. What could be more beautiful than something that binds me closer to you? Though I will attempt to behave in a more gentleman-like manner in the future if you so desire. If not, I am at your disposal.*

KATE GASPED. AND THEN FELT HER FACE HEAT.

I AM TEASING. AS THE DUKE SUGGESTED, I MUST BEHAVE MYSELF *with a greater amount of respect. I hope to see that beautiful red I know is overtaking your creamy skin right now. Until we next see one another and ever after, I am yours.*

WITH ALL MY HEART,
   Logan

SHE HUGGED THE LETTER TO HER HEART FOR MANY MOMENTS, cascading emotions showering through her. Most of them positive, but one niggling doubt plagued her—two, if she were being completely honest. He'd gone to start the paperwork at the duke's request. She didn't like the sound of that. She was growing in confidence that he would have asked her to marry him, but he'd never been given the opportunity to discover such a thing on his own. And that festered in the most insecure part of her heart. And then, the other festering thought involved her own dishonesty, and as no one liked to come face to face with their dishonesty, she pushed it aside. She would fix all the problems she had caused, and then she would tell him all one night, when they could simply laugh about the whole of it.

They spent the week preparing for the ball. Kate had convinced them all to be just that much more bold. When she'd explained to Lucy that being a part of the prince's party meant that a certain fashion was to be expected, she had readily agreed. Charity agreed when Kate had told her she could choose colors, and Grace had always been in agreement. The modiste worked all hours of the day and night that week for them. And when the morning of the ball came, all the dresses arrived.

Kate was almost giddy with excitement. She moved through the rooms. "Sisters. We must arise. Each one of your hairstyles will take well into the afternoon."

"What?" Charity mumbled as she rolled over. "I am not parading about in a hairstyle that requires so many hours to create."

"Oh, you are. Wake up. I've had them bring you a tray. Chocolate." Kate pulled open the blinds, the morning sun shining into the room, filling her with energy. She hadn't seen Lord Dennison in a week, and she was most anxious to see him, and most anxious for him to see their dresses, hers most of all.

When all the sisters were at last sitting at their dressing tables, their maids hard at work, Kate sat at hers. Through the mirror, she smiled at her maid, Hannah. "Are we ready to create a masterpiece?"

"We are always ready."

"Excellent. Then let us begin."

When they were at last on the way to the ball, Kate thought that Charity might leave in a huff as soon as they arrived, so tired she was of the process of dressing for the ball.

Lucy rested a hand on Charity's arm. "An invitation from the prince is a special thing. He particularly might view it as an insult were we to not make such a fuss."

"Hmm." Charity looked out the window. "I console myself knowing that so many I long to converse with will be present. I plan to prove them all wrong, one by one."

"And they flock to you, just for the privilege of being proven wrong on any number of matters." Lucy shrugged, then put her hands on her hips. "Don't forget, we must stay close to Her Grace. Amelia will assist you, Grace. And at no time are we to be alone. The prince's set is not always the safest."

They each nodded. No longer did they underestimate the dangers of some of these activities. They had seen from experience what could happen.

"*Her Lady's Whims and Fancies* should have gone to press already." Kate clasped her hands together.

"I admit, I'm looking forward to seeing everyone's reactions. And hearing their speculation. There's a chance people will actually move to Bath to see the spectacle themselves." Lucy was enjoying this enough, Kate wondered if she'd ever do something similar, perhaps attempt to write a different column.

They arrived at Prince George's Royal Pavilion to a royal welcome. Two lines of red-liveried royal servants stood out in front. Two footmen approached and opened the door, bowing as Kate stepped her first foot out. She ducked low enough that her four feathers could fit out the door. She matched her fictional creation in Bath. Her dress was the brightest green she could manage. Prince George stepped outside the door to greet them, and next to him, a flamboyantly dressed man with feathers on a cap that sat at the side of his head.

Kate's mouth dropped open. "How?"

Her sisters crowded around her. "Is that Lord Dennison?"

"How could that be him?" Grace put her hands at each side of her face.

"Pretend we are perfectly composed." Lucy smiled through her teeth. "Even though I cannot imagine how Lord Dennison is dressed so suspiciously like our pretend man in Bath."

"And what will happen when they run the piece, and everyone again thinks it's him?" Lucy clasped her hands together.

Kate's stomach clenched. "I fear we've just made things worse."

Chapter Eighteen

❦

"Excellent." Logan's grin couldn't grow any wider as he watched Miss Kate approach. "We match." He shook his head. "Uncanny how such a thing could happen." She'd used even the same type of feathers. Her dress was the same color as his colored breeches.

"I admire the use of colors in the breeches. I think it should stick." Lord Ballustrade had joined him and the prince in a different shade of breeches.

"I wasn't certain what to make of your assertion that these sisters would be so impeccably dressed, but they are the perfect choice." Prince George nodded to Logan.

"They are a prime example of why we need a few changes to our law regarding tenants. These sisters are of royal descent, on two lines that we're aware of. And for the last five years, they have been living as tenants, with barely enough to eat."

"What has happened to alter their circumstance?"

"The Duke of Granbury took an active interest in their well-being. And you know Lord Morley? He married the eldest."

"They are lovely indeed."

Logan studied Prince George, and for a moment regretted that he was about to bring the lovely Standish sisters into the presence of one so after a flirtation with anyone in a skirt.

"There is something to this tenant bill. And my support might garner some popularity with the citizens, correct?"

"Yes."

"And it might enable me to take a hit at the dukes? My brothers included?"

"It would protect tenants, certainly, and would require responsible care."

The sisters approached. Each one of them stared at him in such a strange way, he wondered if he stood beside a ghost. When he bowed over Kate's hand, he quirked up a brow. "Do I look that shocking?"

"No. You look perfectly fashion-forward." She wiggled her head to shake her feathers. "We match."

"In more ways than one." He tucked her hand at his side as if he wouldn't ever let her go, which was exactly what he planned.

"How are you wearing feathers? And colored breeches?" She eyed him to his toes, which made him smile. "And more slippers."

"I could say the same of you, with the bright green of your dress. I couldn't be more pleased. Shall we go wow our audience?"

"I guess we shall." Kate tried not to smile—Logan had no idea why—but soon, her grin overtook her face, and he thought her lovelier still.

"You are beautiful. I enjoy your daring fashion sense, but you, Kate, would be beautiful no matter what you wore and no matter how you did your hair."

She didn't answer, but her smile remained as they followed

at the back of their group. Her sisters were on the arms of some of the other more moderately dressed lords, and for the moment, he felt comfortable with their situation.

"Who will be paying attention to Miss Grace?"

"Her Grace. And we will, of course."

"Of course." Logan felt a rising concern. "But that is all? No one else is here to see that you are protected?"

"I feel that their graces should be sufficient, but if you must know, the Duchesses of York and Sussex both take an active interest in our well-being."

"You don't sound as if you appreciate the intrusion."

"I don't. Much."

He laughed. "Well, in that case, we shall attempt to stave off some of their efforts to assist?"

"I'm certain that Charity will be most obliged."

Kate's older sister chatted in between two lords, and they looked to be having a serious discussion.

Kate noticed Logan's attention. "Charity has strong opinions about most things." She pressed her hand into his forearm. "In fact, she might be someone to talk to about your plans for the tenants. She has a comprehensive grasp of most people's opinions about things."

"Does she now?" He considered her. "Would you mind if I pulled myself away from you for one dance to use the time with her?"

"Certainly, you may. We only get the two, anyway."

"Unless I choose to be even more scandalous and use every set for you or a Standish sister."

"I don't think I would complain. And . . . Logan . . ."

Her intimate use of his name made even his feet tingle.

"I loved my flowers."

"And my letter?"

"Yes, and your letter."

"I cannot wait until every evening is ours, until every afternoon spent in a library with my solicitor still meant an afternoon home with you, not sequestered off in a completely different home. Until I wake up to you and go to sleep to you. It's all you, Kate. I've been lonely without you, plain and simple."

Her eyes widened. "Do you really still want me? You are not forced, you know."

"I think His Grace might feel otherwise, and I'd venture to guess Lord Morley might echo his sentiments, but Kate . . . My love for you . . . it is dictated by no one but my own heart."

"But we have time . . . to consider, to still know each other."

Logan studied her face. A new fear flickered across her features. "Do you need that time?" He watched, waiting. His fear resurfacing. In a way, being forced to act had been a relief to him. But not if Kate felt hesitant in her feelings. "Do you . . . still wish to be with me?"

Their conversation became more and more hushed, their steps slower as the others moved on ahead, and their faces intent and close. "I do. I long to be with you. But I . . . I want us to *choose* this."

His breath left in a slow relief as his shoulders relaxed. "Then we are of one mind. About yet another thing." His fingers rose and toyed with her feathers. "Is it possible that you and I considered the fashions, chose the most forward-thinking possibility we could think of, and wore it on the same day, only to match precisely with each other?"

"It is possible." She smiled.

"And you know we will attract all manner of attention."

"Yes, I know."

"And you know we will be written about in that heathen paper, *Her Lady's Whims and Fancies*."

"I—I know."

"And you would still like to enter those doors up there, to be announced . . . together?"

"I would."

"You might have to marry me after all the talk this will cause."

"There's that phrase, 'have to,' again."

Logan smiled at her, but he knew of what he spoke. "Kate . . ."

"I love it when you use my first name." She placed a hand at the side of his face. And he abhorred gloves so much in that moment, he wished to rip hers from her fingers. "Let them talk. I have no cares for any other than you."

He drank in the sparkle in her eyes and the fullness of her mouth. "I would kiss you right now if I hadn't already got myself in enough trouble."

She laughed. "Best save that for later."

"Oh, ho! Then I most certainly shall."

They moved closer to the entrance. The emcee called out the next set of names.

By the time they were announced and actually at the ball, Logan had almost grown tired of it. The moment they stepped into the room, every eye naturally turned in his direction, but the gasps and the smiles and the excitement in the room were far more pronounced than he expected.

Kate was immediately surrounded by women. As he stepped aside to make room, he called over, "Do you know these women?"

She just smiled and then turned her attention to the excited chatter.

He wanted none of that and so, reluctantly, he left her to stand with Prinny and his set.

They eyed the group of ladies. "Do you suppose she could

bring them all in our direction?" Lord Bester, the man who had Miss Lucy on his arm, nodded toward the ladies.

"I don't know. They seem unapproachable at the moment," Logan said.

"Yes, why must they travel in flocks?"

"I will never pretend to understand the mind of a woman, not entirely." Lord Ballustrade joined them at his side. "But your Miss Kate. She is a stunning woman. How did you know she had such uncommonly gifted fashion sense?"

"I could only but briefly suspect such a thing when I saw her at the church. She is quite a paragon of her own making. See the women? They seek out her fashion advice."

"Uncanny."

"Yes, I've said the same."

They moved about the room together, the prince laughing and puffing out his own cravat, the Creation, while discussing his wildly floral purple breeches. "We've created a sensation," he said. Logan looked about the room. Most people looked in their direction. He'd venture a guess that every conversation involved them at that moment.

"What shall we do with such attention?" Logan asked.

"Pardon me?" Ballustrade took a sip from a wine cup he'd grabbed from a passing servant.

"Do you ever wonder how much good you could do if you exerted yourself in the House of Lords? If we worked together on a bill?"

Ballustrade looked at him like he'd grown a peacock to join the feathers on his head. "I spend calculated effort attempting never to attend a meeting."

"But consider if you did . . ." He stopped talking. Lord Ballustrade's attention had already wandered, and Logan knew swaying him to anything other than his focus on fashion would be useless.

At last, the music began, and he went in search of Kate for their first set.

But she had moved out onto the floor with another, a weaselly baron with a boring tweed jacket and bumbling feet. Her gaze met his, which was full of questions, but her helpless response reminded him that he hadn't asked her for the set. "Of all the . . ." He gritted his teeth and waited at the side of the dance floor for the music to end.

A group of women stood not too far behind him, and their chatter was loud enough to reach everyone's ears, his particularly, as they discussed his Kate.

"She is the very best person to go to for fashion advice. How does she always know the fashions before they appear in *Whims and Fancies?*"

"I know! It's like she wrote them herself, she is so savvy. I asked her about her feathers, and she said that she and Lord Dennison didn't even plan such a thing. They just know."

The others giggled and continued discussing something but moved out of earshot. He considered their words. How did Kate seem to always know? Why was she wearing the precise descriptions that were found in *Her Lady's Whims and Fancies?* He shook his head. And she'd been rather destitute just a few months' past, if the rumors were accurate. So how would she know, being so far from London and so far from any of society's elite? He couldn't account for it. Perhaps she'd been a regular reader for all this time; perhaps she searched catalogues? Ackermans? They did say they'd had regular visits from the duchesses with last season's gowns. He had no way of knowing. A tiny suspicion worked its way into his thoughts. How could she possibly know?

Another group of women passed behind him. "They are saying the *Whims and Fancies* editor is here in Brighton. Else how would they know so much about the fashions right now?

We are at the edge of fashion. Perhaps they'll write about me!"
The group passed by, each voice blending into another.

How indeed did they know so much about him particularly,
even here in Brighton? How had they described his cravat so
carefully? How had they known the details for the wedding so
intimately? The editor was here in Brighton, perhaps at the
Royal Pavilion even now. His gaze traveled over the group.
What man here doubled as a fashion expert for *The Morning
Star*? He would have thought someone from his set, but not one
of them would have portrayed his cravat as anything less than
glorious. No, this person had a vendetta, or a strong opposition
to creativity at the neckline . . . or some other bitterness of
soul. He gave up searching. No one was going to pop out at
him. He laughed. What would they say about the matching
feathers?

At last, the dance ended, but then Kate was swept into the
arms of another. Logan opened and closed his hands three
times before he could breathe normally. What was she doing?

Julia stepped up beside him. "Why aren't you dancing with
Miss Kate?"

"She keeps dancing with others."

"Did you ask her for a set?"

"No." He ground his teeth together. "I just assumed, and
rightly so, that she would want to dance with her almost
fiancé."

"Never assume, brother. Never assume." She watched Kate
glance in their direction twice. "I wonder how many sets she
has lined up already for her evening."

"Do you think she saved any for me?" His voice sounded
more pathetic than he meant, but the ball was going to be one
long, bleak lesson in endurance if he did not get to hold Kate or
dance with Kate, or even talk with Kate for the duration.

"She might have saved you the supper set?" Julia shrugged.

"How would we know unless we ask her?" Her smile held sympathy, but Logan knew she was laughing inside at him, and he didn't appreciate it, especially not when someone came to collect her for a dance.

He crossed his arms and waited out another dance, his face probably glowering, but he didn't even care.

Chapter Nineteen

K ate went from one man to the next, unsure of how to respond to a man she'd already agreed to dance a set with. She hadn't known what Logan's plans would be. He hadn't asked for any sets. She knew he wanted to dance with her, but she'd already agreed to others. He couldn't really dance every set with her, no matter what he boasted. She had kept the supper set open.

And in between most sets, she was surrounded again by women. They all wanted to understand the feathers. She had pointed out they all wore feathers, but she and they knew that Kate's were more outlandish, more garish, and even more beautiful. So she had shared what she could, how she had ordered them and been saving them for just such a moment. They were enamored with the bright color of her gown. They even wanted to see her slippers, which she now regretted were her simple ball slippers. The bells would have been a fun adornment to share.

With any luck, all of this attention elsewhere would help

Logan. With any luck, he could be spared at least some of the attention *Whims and Fancies* and society were bound to send his way when it was discovered that the very same outfit was seen in Bath and in Brighton. She cringed whenever she thought of it. How could such a thing be? How?

At a small break in between people, Lucy stood at her side. "You better just confess about the whole thing."

And Kate knew she was right. The more she tried to fix things, the further broken they became. So with those heavy thoughts, she determined to enjoy the rest of her evening and break the news to Logan tomorrow.

At last, the supper set arrived. She turned down four lords before Logan could make his way over to her. He pulled her into his arms, closer than was allowed, as the music to a waltz began.

She laughed into his grumpy face. "Good to see you, Lord Dennison."

"And now I'm lord again, am I?"

"How has the ball been for you?"

He grunted and spun the two of them around. But his frown didn't stay for long—soon, the corners curled up, and he was laughing. "You are a superb dancer."

"Thank you."

He twirled them. "See, no matter what I do, you follow as though you have wings on your toes." He tipped his head down. "You don't, do you?"

"No wings, or bells, either."

"Ah, you wish you'd worn the bells."

"I certainly do, but these slippers will have to do." She smiled. "I'm sorry to have missed so many sets with you, but see, we have the longest four all to ourselves."

"Before and after supper, which is also mine, correct?"

"Correct."

His eyes moved about to take in the edges of the ballroom. "People are talking."

"You knew they would."

"Yes. I find it odd, don't you? That *Whims and Fancies* would know so many details about us, particularly here in Brighton."

"Do you?"

"Yes. There is talk that the artist and writers are right here."

Kate laughed, nervously. "Then I hope they are getting a good look at my best side."

Logan appreciated her humor, she could tell, but something was bothering him. "Did Prince George agree to help?"

"Yes, he is all in, and I think I owe his agreement in part to you."

"Me?"

"Yes, you and your sisters, coming from such a difficult time, tenants yourselves and then walking in with such a pleasing array of clothing. It really touched Prince George in just the right way."

"Then all is well, isn't it? You are benefitting from all the attention; you will be able to begin work on important things. You can dress how you want. Envious position, honestly." She watched him, her hope rising.

"Yes." He pulled her closer. "None of that matters compared to the happiness I feel with you. I can hardly wait for us to become married ourselves. You will love my estate. And I love staying here in Brighton. We will go and be and do whatever we wish, and we will be together."

Kate relaxed her shoulders and enjoyed the love that Logan was showering down on her, for she wasn't certain she'd ever feel that same approving warmth from him again. "It all sounds like heaven."

"And it will be ours. Kate, come. I can hold back my words no longer; let us go find a quiet room. I have something I wish to ask you." His face was earnest, his eyes full of love, and Kate ached to hear what he would say, yearned for it like she had an orange when they'd had nothing to eat, but she had to prevent him. Tonight was not the night. This was not the moment. She had to admit to him all she'd done.

"Come tomorrow. Come as soon as you wake. We'll go for a walk."

He struggled for a moment. His eyes conflicted, his steps slowed. And for a moment, she thought he was going to drag her off the floor anyway, else get down on his knees right there in front of everyone. But he nodded. "Very well." He was quiet for a moment more, then he pressed his lips to the top of her forehead. "I love you, Kate. I'd wait ten years if I had to."

Tears sprung to her eyes, and she didn't even try to hide them. "I love you, too."

THE NEXT MORNING, KATE WAS STILL IN BED, PUTTING OFF her conversation with Logan for as long as she could, when Grace bobbed into the room. "Lord Dennison is here to see you. One of the servants put him in the library."

Kate shot up out of her bed. "Oh no!"

Grace watched her for a moment. "Your drawings?"

She scrambled up and grabbed a morning dress. "Here, help me put this on."

While Grace threw It up over her head and fumbled with the buttons, Kate ran a brush through her hair. "I left it all out during the night. My drawings, the plates, everything." Her heart sank. She was about to tell him, but he would never know that. To stumble upon her secret first was the worst possible scenario.

Kate didn't even bother putting her hair up. She raced through the family wing, down the stairs in her bare feet, through the main hall, down the other corridor, and into the library, breathing hard.

As she'd dreaded, Logan stood behind the desk, going through the fashion plates she'd left on top. With any luck, he wouldn't know they were for *The Morning Star.*

"So, you're *Her Lady's Whims and Fancies?*" His face was blank, but his eyes showed hurt. And she wished to wipe away the distrust. She wished to wipe it from her memory. Her heart tore in two at the sight.

"I am. Sometimes. Please, before you start thinking anything, we need to talk about this."

"What do you mean sometimes?"

"I recently started. And I'm not the only one. Another has been posting opinions lately as well."

"But it was you? My cravat? The Cravat Magician?"

She thought of the night everyone had made fun because of her plate. She'd made it so much more difficult for him to make a difference right when he had started to set goals and make plans. "I didn't know you then."

He closed his eyes. "And after that?"

"I kept attempting to show you in a new light. It didn't work. And then I tried to distract the readers from you by giving them something else to focus on. And . . ." She hated to say this next part. What could she possibly do to prevent what was about to happen?

"And?"

"And we created a new person, a fake . . . lord who dressed in the most outlandish manner possible. I even wore a matching type of outfit to give believability to the story should people read it, and placed him in Bath."

Logan blinked five times before he said anything. "I don't understand."

"But you showed up in the same clothes, the same imagined up plate we had created, and I matched you, it. I could never have guessed such a thing would happen."

He nodded, slowly.

"And it will be delivered to all the homes tomorrow. And then the other writer and artist, whoever it might be, will be certain to say that another sighting of the same clothing happened right here in Brighton." She wrung her hands together, his stoic and unreadable face making her feel worse and worse. "And so in the act of attempting to deflect some of the attention, in trying to create a new fashion obsession, I only made it worse."

He stared at her for a very long time, long enough that her legs trembled beneath her, and she moved to sit. "I'm sorry. I wanted to tell you. I've been plagued with unhappiness about my terrible dishonesty. You had to know this before you asked me to marry you." She choked on the last word. "If you still wish to."

His gaze shot up to her eyes. Then he held up a drawing. "And you were going to send this in?" He held a picture of the two of them, side by side with their matching outfits. She'd even included their faces.

She nodded. "And I was going to quit."

He read the words she already knew by heart. "Dear Reader. It is with great reluctance that I must turn in my resignation as your fashion plate designer and writer. As much as I love to share bits of fun from everyone we know, I feel that to some, my actions have been harmful. Please accept my deepest apologies and remember that each of us is more than what we wear. We are real people with hearts and dreams and desires. Sometimes, the best dressed among us are the most interesting, but do they have the truest hearts? In the case of the Cravat Magician, I would say that his heart is far grander even than his creativity with his apparel."

His hand shook, and he dropped the paper. "And you think this? This . . . will solve all our problems?" He lifter their image again, showing her. "Don't send this."

She could hardly look at him, with his eyes turning steely, his mouth pressing together, his hands stiffening.

"I . . . I tried. I wanted them to focus on someone else. I tried to fix what I'd done."

He shook his head. "The attention was not the problem . . ." He cleared his throat. "In and of itself, it was a nuisance, but nothing I couldn't fix. I was using it to my advantage with the prince and the others of his set."

She thought she might be relieved at what he said, but something about his face made her suspect that more was coming.

He gripped the table. "The problem here is that . . . is that you are just like Olivia." His eyes flashed. "You said things, acted one way, but really, in your heart, you are someone else entirely. And I cannot . . . I cannot even trust who you claim to be now. You used me. Would you have ever told me? Or just continued to write about me, your husband?" He shook his head. "I know I said I would do right by you, but as you seem in no hurry to be entrapped by me, I think I'm going to need some time." He nodded his head and then made his way around the desk to leave the room.

"Is there nothing else to say?"

"Is there?" He stopped, waiting. "Have you any other reason for your actions?"

She sighed. "No. I'm sorry, Logan. If there's anything more I can do to make it right, I will."

"No. Don't do anything else." He lifted his chin and walked out of the room.

As soon as he was gone, Kate's face fell into her hands, and she cried out all her hopes that she'd ever see him smiling into her face again.

Chapter Twenty

Logan lifted *The Morning Star* and read Kate's last article for *Whims and Fancies* for the thousandth time in the last three weeks. He ran his finger along their faces. He chuckled at her last statement. "Because I'm not certain you will believe that two people could show up with something so new and so alike on the same evening without planning it first, here is the evidence. Those who know us will not be surprised."

He rubbed his face and forehead with his hands.

A knock at his opened door jerked him to his feet.

"Easy there. Archer said I could just come in." The Duke of Granbury stood in the doorway.

Logan fell back into his chair. "I assume you are here to challenge me to a duel?"

His Grace laughed. "May I?" He pulled out a chair to give himself some legroom.

Logan nodded.

"I am come for no such reason. But you look a mess. If *Whims and Fancies* could see you now."

"Stop." Logan eyed him for a moment and then sat up straighter. "But now you're here. Have you been sufficiently convinced to support our tenant bill?"

The duke waved his hand. "Yes, yes. I threw my hat in at the very first."

"Ah yes, you did. Thank you."

"It's a generous and important move. I hope some of those stodgy Tories will lend their votes."

"I as well." Logan leaned back in his chair, wondering why His Grace had come.

"I've come back to London for the rest of the season."

"Oh?"

"Yes, Morley—well, the Morleys—have joined me, and the sisters."

Logan grunted, but his heart thundered through him.

"With so many returning from Brighton, we thought it smart to introduce them to the wider associations that can be had in town."

"Did you?"

"Oh, come off it, man. I'm here to invite you to dinner. You don't have to pretend you're not thrilled she's come." The duke stood.

"Does she want to see me?"

His Grace stared at him long and hard, so long Logan thought he might not answer. "She does."

Logan's breath left in a great, relieving gust.

"But she won't admit it."

He nodded, slowly. "So . . . where does that leave me?"

"I think you'd best talk to her about that. But look smart. Bring Lady Julia. Tuesday next."

"Thank you."

His Grace nodded, and then left the room.

Kate. In London. He stood. Then he sat. He'd been so angry

last they'd spoken. Perhaps a note, a card? Flowers? "Yes." He pulled his bell pull.

"Yes, my lord."

"Send some flowers to Lord Morley's townhome, addressed to Miss Kate Standish. Sign it, 'With all my love.'"

"Yes, Your Grace. Any particular kinds?"

"Kinds? Oh yes, certainly. Every kind. Make it the most outlandishly, mismatched bunch she's ever seen. Eye-poppingly dreadful."

"Yes, my lord."

He paced the room. Kate. In London. Each one of those sisters would get snatched up so quickly, they might have three weddings this year. He sat back down. Might his be one of them? Oh, he hoped so.

He had plenty of reasons to be hurt. She hadn't confided in him. She'd caused some difficulty. But she'd also paved the way for some of his notoriety to aid him in his new efforts. When he'd considered the timing, she would have sent the first cravat drawing right after he'd insulted her dreadfully. Could he blame her for having the most ill feelings for him at the time? He really couldn't. Especially now that it had been so long since he'd laid eyes on her at all. He couldn't be anything but anxious to see her, to hold her in his arms, to kiss her once again. To marry the woman—oh, he'd give anything to marry the woman. Swallow any amount of pride, apologize for not accepting her apology, whatever it took.

He dug through his drawer. A small, folded paper—a letter from Miss Grace.

"Kate wrote *Whims and Fancies* because she is afraid to be hungry ever again. She loves you. And we're all miserable until you two make things right."

He pressed the missive to his lips. "She loves me."

His appointment to ride though Hyde Park called to him.

He must dress. This crowd was his more conservative Oxford bunch. They'd joined with him on the efforts to support tenants. And he found their conversation invigorating, and their friendship true and sensible. But their clothing was so dull, it almost hurt his eyes.

WHEN HE WAS AT LAST ON HIS HORSE RIDING AMONGST friends, he realized that life was about to get sweeter than it had ever been. If she would have him, if they could have but a moment to converse, perhaps they could make something of themselves, make a life together.

Lord Connolly called over to him, "At least you've not been parading about in the ridiculous color choices of earlier this season."

Logan laughed, and the others did, too, but he shifted uncomfortably in his saddle. He liked the ridiculous color choices.

"Who knows, Connolly, but I might bring back the feathers."

"Oh please, Dennison. I've seen enough men in feathers."

"Have you? Well, what exactly would you like me to bring into fashion?"

They didn't seem to have an opinion about fashion at all, so he turned back in his saddle and smiled. How could they abide such grey and black and white and tan lives? Where was the fun in that?

"What in the blazes?" Connolly squinted his eyes at something very brightly colored up ahead.

Logan followed his gaze and then laughed out loud. "If you'll excuse me, gentlemen." He dipped his head in their direction and kicked his horse. Kate's clothing was more delightfully outrageous the closer he came. When he was close enough, he slipped off his horse, left him to graze close by, and approached a very vibrantly dressed Kate. He tried not to laugh, but she was almost ridiculously attired, the purple and the orange and the yellows clashing in such a discordant mix, it almost hurt his eyes. "What is this?"

"It's all the rage, haven't you heard?"

"I must have missed this part of the rage."

"Pity."

His friends approached on their horses. Sounds of them shifting and pawing the ground behind him made him equal parts protective and irritated. But before he could say anything, Kate shook her head. "I've got this," she whispered. Then she turned to them and curtseyed. "Pleasure to see you gentlemen."

Conolly tipped his hat to her, and the others snickered.

"I'm going to give you an inside scoop on a bet going on at Whites."

A few more perked up their ears.

"Yesiree. There's some speculation about whether or not Lord Dennison and Miss Kate Standish will ever forgive one another." She turned wide and hopeful eyes in his direction.

"Yes, we will." Logan stepped closer to her, wanting nothing more than to pull her into his arms and kiss her senseless. "So, why don't you gentlemen go place your bets. I think odds are against us, according to that pessimistic running."

They took off with their horses, shouting thanks over their shoulders.

Then she lowered herself to her knees.

"What are you doing? Stand up." He checked to make certain none of the departing lords had looked back to notice.

"Oh, fine. But I have something to ask you, and you're making me nervous."

Joy hammered through him. "Have you now? Well, out with it then."

She held up Matilda's ring. "I even have a ring for myself, for now."

"Is this? May I?" Logan studied it. "This is incredible. This could have been touched by William the Conqueror himself."

"And Matilda."

"Yes, quite."

"And still, I haven't had a chance to ask my question." She lowered to her knees again.

He looked around at a new group of people gathering. "You're drawing a crowd."

"Do you think it's the dress?"

"Or it has something to do with you down on your knees. Or it's the hat." The purple feathers that rose out of the top of her hat shimmered from her movement.

"I care not what they think. Logan, I can't live without you. I'm so terribly sorry about *Whims and Fancies*. I didn't write any of the things that came after we became . . . close. None of it. I should have told you, but it was just so difficult, and I kept trying to fix things. We made up a fictional person. A paragon of fashion in Bath. And then you showed up as him."

His smile grew.

"You know all this, I know. I told you, but just in case you forgot . . ."

"Yes." Logan pulled Kate to her feet again and tucked her hand in the crook of his arm. "Can we walk?"

"Don't think you're getting out of hearing my question."

"I wouldn't miss it." He patted her hand. "After I read your message in *Whims and Fancies*, I paid a visit to His Grace."

"Oh?"

"Yes, quite. And he told me the sordid details of your time as the fashion plate creator and writer of *Her Lady's Whims and Fancies*."

"And?"

"And I have to say, I feel a bit humbled to be in your presence."

"Stop."

"No, really. You have become the female Beau Brummel of our time. Think of the power you have. If you wished it, everyone would be wearing brown."

"Brown?"

"Certainly."

Kate considered him. "So am I forgiven?"

Logan's eyes turned serious. "I cannot stay angry with you. Shortly after my departure from Brighton, I already regretted my words."

"You've made a good name for yourself, I hear."

"Yes, the prince is aiding us. And there is a good chance we can make a difference with these ideas."

"I'm so happy for you."

"Yes, yes. I am happy as well. But I thought you came to talk of other things?"

"Oh, certainly. I did, yes." She knelt down again. This time, he let her.

"Lord Dennison, will you please, please, please take me to be your wife?"

He pulled her back to her feet. "As proposals go, that was pretty mild."

"Would you like me to add another please?"

"No, please. Do not do such a thing." He raised one of her hands to his lips. "My dear Kate. I need you in my life. I've been a cad to stay away so long. I love you with all that I have, and beg you to please, please, please be my wife." He tried to push it away, but his heart shuddered with fear, a small flash of Olivia's refusal sweeping through his memory.

"Yes. Oh yes. Yes, yes. I will." Kate stepped into his

embrace. "Yes, I can think of nothing that matters more to me than to simply be your wife."

Logan stared down into her face, shining all the love he could imagine. "My dear Kate." He pressed his lips to hers, which were soft and warm, and spent far too little time there. "I have papers already drawn up. We have a special license. We can marry whenever you would like."

"We need at least a month for the dresses to be made, and that's if the modiste has time and makes only our clothes. And to reserve the church. I presume we can find a day. But flowers. And wouldn't it be lovely if we could host the ball at the castle? Those renovations won't be finished for sixty days, at least. What about three months?"

He sighed. "Would it could be tomorrow. But I should have known you would want to design the dresses."

"Naturally."

He placed her hand back on his arm. "Then we shall plan it in three months' time."

Kate's attention seemed to wander.

Logan cleared his throat once, twice, and then she looked back in his direction. "Might I make a small request?" he asked.

"What might that be?"

"That this particular dress not make a reappearance."

She looked down at her skirts. "Do you know, I forgot I had this on?"

"I can't understand how you would."

"I did! But it did the trick. You couldn't possibly ignore me while wearing this."

"And that was your main goal? To catch my attention?"

"That, my dear Logan, is always my main goal."

They walked along, his smile twitching at his lips, trying to come out for so long, until she laughed into the sky. "Are you as happy as I?"

"I don't think anyone could ever be as happy as we."

"No one."

They walked a minute more, then he frowned. "Where am I taking you?"

"I'm staying at Morley's townhome."

"Oh, of course . . . And you're here in the park alone?"

"Not exactly."

Logan paused and looked around them. Then squinted his eyes into a copse of trees. "Is that?"

Grace's giggling made it to their ears, and then she and Lucy and Charity stepped out followed by June.

"What! You are all here?"

"Of course. We couldn't let Kate come propose by herself." Grace stepped closer and up on tiptoes. "Welcome to the family." She kissed his cheek.

Lucy and Charity did the same.

"Thank you. I feel I have just entered a very exclusive club."

"You have. Not everyone can be a part of the Sisters of Sussex."

"No indeed."

The Duke's Second Chance Chapter One

The duchess's labor had started in the carriage while returning to their London townhome. Perhaps her pinched face and general malaise during the earlier parts of the day should have clued the duke in that all was not right, but she gave no complaint, and now he was left only to wish she had expressed a word or two of her condition. He'd carried her himself into her room, her gowns wet through. At last on her bed, he was relieved she would be in the hands of someone more experienced than he who knew how to care for her. But as he brushed the hair from her forehead, as he gazed on his beloved's face, he couldn't bear to part, not yet, not with her in the utmost misery.

Gerald clasped his wife's hands in his own, hoping the strength of his love for her would scare away the pain.

Her face pinched, and she doubled over, large drops of sweat falling off her forehead. "Don't leave!"

"I'm here. Our illustrious midwife will have to unleash her dragon claws on me before I leave."

That brought a tiny laugh from his wife which gratified

Gerald to no end. He tried to keep up a form of banter with Camilla who was clenched in the pains of childbirth, but in truth, if she wasn't gripping him so tightly, everyone in the room would see the trembling in his own limbs. She cried out. "It's getting worse. Is this supposed to happen?" Her eyes, wide with terror, made him frantic.

"Someone do something!" He had tried to find his deep barreling voice but the order came out more of a squeak than anything.

The midwife sidled up to him, "Pardon me, Your Grace. If I may?" She attempted to separate their hands, but he and Camilla resisted, gripping tighter. She continued, "She is doing wonderfully. Her body is performing just as we would expect it to. Everything is progressing as it should. Soon you will have a new baby."

Camilla rolled toward him onto her side, moaning and writhing on the bed.

"If I might?" The midwife gently tried again to pry their fingers apart, but Camilla clung to him. "No." Her no came out as a long drawn out syllable and he almost stepped back in fear. But her grip on him offered no mercy, and no movement.

"I'm here." He stated his determination to remain at her side. Though even to himself, his tone sounded less sure.

He hesitated one more moment, then Camilla screamed as though she were on a torture rack and released his hands, clutching instead the soothing cool fingers of their midwife, her cooing tones soothed Gerald as much as Camilla.

Gerald scooted further away. The door opened behind him. "Your Grace. I came as soon as I could."

Gerald turned. "Dr. Miller. Thank you for coming."

The doctor held the door open for him. "I'm presuming you were on your way out?"

Gerald nodded. "Yes, quite." Just for a moment he would step into the hallway.

His wife turned eyes to him, beautiful, shining eyes full of love. "I shall be finished shortly they tell me." Then her body clenched again and she curled into a ball. "Make it stop. Please make this stop."

"I love you, Camilla."

She waved him away, clenched in apparent agony.

The doctor shooed him out the door and before it closed firmly behind him, Gerald heard a quiet, "I love you too." Gerald leaned up against it, breathing heavily. What a daft thing to do, impregnate his wife. What in the blazes was he thinking doing such a thing to them both? He closed his eyes, her scream audible through the thick door.

"Oh this will not do." His friend's voice lessened the strain that wound inside Gerald like a tight net.

Gerald whipped his eyes open, a welcoming smile interrupting the pain of his moment. "Cousin Morley. I've ruined her. She'll never forgive me, I'm certain, and she's in the most incredible pain."

Another scream interrupted. The door flung open and a maid ran out, carrying linens and a bucket. The door shut firmly after her.

Morley gripped his shoulder. "Come, man. This is not the place for husbands. Wives always seem just fine after it's all over."

"I don't know. She seemed determined I stay by her. I'm taking a break." He swallowed.

"No, they say that at first, but what woman wants you to see her like that? It's only going to get worse. You should have seen my sister's household. The whole place was in a upheaval, everyone thinking their lady was going to fire them all."

Morley considered his friends words. "And when it was over, she was recovered?"

"Certainly. She was in the best of moods, gave them all an increase in pay." Morley put an arm across his shoulder. "Come. We don't belong anywhere near her. It's off to the study with your fine brandy."

Gerald nodded. "Indeed. That sounds like just the thing." He hesitated a moment more and then allowed the good will of his dearest friend to lead him along to a brighter manner in which to pass the time.

The farther away from her bedroom, the more the fibers of worry lessened, and Gerald told himself his wife was in the best of hands, that women gave birth all the time and that surely she would be well. He pushed away a persistent, niggling worry that something terrible was happening, pushed it as far as he could. For just as his friend said, what more could he do? She would be well soon enough and he could meet his son or daughter. Their lives would continue as before.

Morley made himself comfortable in the study as he always did. Leaning back in his favorite chair, he said, "Remember when we convinced Joe that his cow was about to give birth?"

Gerald snorted, almost losing his mouthful of brandy. "Clueless Joe believed us, with not a bull in sight on their estate."

Morley laughed and raised his cup in the air. "To Joe."

"To Joe."

They downed their cups, and Morley poured two new ones. "Thanks for being here."

"Would I miss the best thing you've ever done?"

Gerald eyed him with suspicion. "That sounds very sentimental..."

"We hope. If your child is anything like *Her* Grace, then we're sure of you doing a service to society..."

"And if the child's like me?"

"Then we've just inflicted society with another Campbell, and I don't know how I feel about that."

"Being a Campbell yourself."

"Precisely. I know what a pox we are on the land."

Gerald downed his second cup, grateful for a reason to laugh. "Tell me cousin. Will there ever be another Campbell in your life?"

"If my mother has anything to say on the matter."

"And what say you? Surely someone has caught your eye?"

Morley looked away, his face drawn in an uncharacteristic frown. "I've found women to be nothing more than a silly, grappling means of entrapment." He coughed. "Present wives excluded."

Gerald sympathized with his friend. Finding a woman to marry should not be so difficult. He felt supremely lucky, blessed, in his marriage to Camilla. They had fallen in love straight away, both of them happy to pursue a courtship, their parents pleased, society approving, but he knew it wasn't so easy for most people.

"Come, man. I shall devote the next bit of my life to making you the happiest of men."

Morley held up his hands and shook his head. "Assistance not necessary. In fact, quite unwelcome."

"Think nothing of it. I want you just as happily situated as I am, for marriage has brought nothing but the best of feelings. Today's activities aside, naturally."

A man cleared his throat in the doorway.

The doctor, at last. Gerald rushed forward, shaking his hand. "Are you the first to congratulate me?"

Morley arrived at his side, his face pinched.

The doctor looked tired, older by ten years since he'd arrived. "Your Grace."

Alarm spiked through Gerald. "What is it? Camilla? Is she well? The baby?"

Dr. Miller shook his head. "We could have never known the baby would be sitting backward, that the duchess would bleed like she did..." Dr. Miller rubbed his head with a shaking hand. "I'm sorry, Your Grace."

Gerald grasped the man by the shoulders, trying to clear his mind, trying to shake the brandy from his cloudy thinking. "Speak sense man."

"We lost her." The words left the doctor's mouth in a slow motion, his face falling into a sick despairing expression.

"What?" He turned from Dr. Miller and ran to his wife's bedroom, his heart willing the doctor's words to erase. Holding his breath, wishing to erase the last hour. He pushed open the door, a maid falling to the floor on the other side as he rushed to his wife's side, lifting her frame into his arms, her sickly white skin still warm to his touch. He clutched her to his chest. "Camilla."

Her arms hung limp at her side. He lifted them, holding them close to his chest. Her neck drooped, her head hanging uselessly at her shoulders. "No." He lifted her head so it was upright. "Camilla. Can you hear me?"

Someone stood at his side. And a familiar hand clasped his shoulder. "Gerald."

He shook his head.

"Gerald."

He clenched his eyes tight, blocking out the world, blocking out Camilla's lack of response, blocking out the friend at his side, even the doctor's words.

And then a cry broke the silence. A baby's cry.

Gerald's eyes fluttered open, and his heart pounded. Turning his head, he clutched Camilla tighter. A baby cried in the arms of their midwife. He could not make sense of this infant. Why was there a baby in the room making all that racket? Didn't they know that his Camilla needed help? He blinked, trying to understand what he was seeing. Morley stepped to the side of the midwife and took the child into his arms. "Looks like you have an heir."

And then everything seemed to speed up and race past him. And he made sense of his situation. "Take him out."

"Pardon me, Your Grace?" The midwife seemed hard of hearing all of a sudden.

"Out. Now. I don't want to lay eyes on the creature who was the cause of Camilla's death."

"Oh, but surely this slip of a thing had nothing—"

Morley placed a hand on her arm, shook his head, and the woman wisely held her tongue.

Then Morley said some nonsense about the nursemaid before it was once again blessedly quiet. He released Camilla's dear body and placed her precisely the way she liked to sleep, on her side, with one hand under her cheek. Then he pulled the blankets up to her chin and tucked her in carefully. He was surprised by the tears that fell from his eyes, wetting everything. His body shuddered, his breaths coming with great effort, fighting against a new tightness that filled his chest.

He stood, unsure what to do. Did he stay by Camilla? Yes. He sat back down. But what more did she require of him? She was at rest, the ultimate rest. He stood. Who took care of such things? Her burial. Someone had to let Camilla's parents know. He covered his eyes, the wetness there again surprising him.

"Gerald."

Morley stood at his side.

Gerald turned again to his oldest friend. And the man who stood a hand taller than him, pulled him into his broad chest and hugged him like a young lad. And Gerald clung to him until his body quit shaking. Then he stepped back, at last able to take in a full breath. "What is to be done?"

"I'll take care of it. We'll notify everyone who must know. We will make arrangements for her burial."

Gerald turned away. Camilla already looked so far away. Her lifeless form had nothing to do with the vibrant soul who used to inhabit it. The light that had shone through her eyes, that broadened her smile, the laugh that had started deep in her belly and bubbled overflowing into a great and joyful music... everything that made Camilla who she was, was gone. And Gerald didn't know where she went. He reached down and placed his hand on her forehead, seeking the last bit of warmth left, finding precious little, he whispered, "Goodbye, my love, my dearest Camilla."

And allowed Morley to lead him out of the room.

READ the rest of this story HERE.